Funny as a Dead Relative

Funny as a Dead Relative

A Kimmey Kruse Mystery

Susan Rogers Cooper

St. Martin's Press
New York

Library of Congress Cataloging-in-Publication Data
Cooper, Susan Rogers.
    Funny as a dead relative / Susan Rogers Cooper.
      p.   cm.
    "A Thomas Dunne book."
    ISBN 0-312-11438-9
    1. Women comedians—Texas—Fiction.
  2. Family—Texas—Fiction. I. Title.
PS3553.O6235F82   1994
813'.54—dc20   94-21122
                                      CIP

First edition: October 1994

10 9 8 7 6 5 4 3 2 1

*This book is dedicated
to the memory of
Allen C. Cooper,
the best coon-ass
wing shot in
Jefferson County, Texas*

Acknowledgments

No book is an island, and this one is no exception. I would like to thank comic Robin Wilson for allowing me to stand around and laugh during her defensive-driving course and giving me all the insider goodies, and Craig Shilling, director of Austin's Comedy Defensive Driving, for all the help and information. I would also like to thank Randall P. Whatley and Harry Jannise for their insight into the Cajun language, Martha Ferguson for information about old Port Arthur, and Erin Fitzgerald for allowing me a walk through her "funny file."

A special thanks to the Black Shoes—Jan Grape, Barbara Burnett Smith, and Jeff Abbott—whose insights (and abilities to read the same stuff over and over and over) are much welcome. As always, thanks to my wonderful editor Ruth Cavin and to Don and Evin Cooper for putting up with it all.

A very special thank-you to my Port Arthur clan—Doris Cooper, Frances Romero, and Dorothy "Aunt Boo" Crosby—for the clippings and the endless miles of showing me this and explaining that and taking me here and driving me there. But mostly just for being family, which is what this book is all about.

Author's Note

There are some readers whose high school and college French teachers would have heart attacks at the French usage in this book. Let me just say that the French used in this book is "seventeenth-century French," brought to this country by LaSalle and other French-speaking explorers. When Quebec, the first permanent French settlement in North America, was founded in 1608, "standard French" did not exist. At that time, there were fifteen dialects of French spoken in France. Today's French, "francien," was spoken in and around Paris and has now become "pure" French. The Cajun French is based on a seventeenth-century French dialect, and has been influenced over the years by Spanish and English.

Funny
as a
Dead
Relative

I LOOKED AT MY REFLECTION IN THE MIRROR. THAT I DID NOT burst into tears upon seeing it is proof of my great personal restraint and fortitude. There is nothing in this world worse than bad hair. And I had a gigantic case of it. It was, of course, my own fault. Word of warning: When in Pittsburgh, Pennsylvania, or anywhere, for that matter, never go to a hair salon called Chez Butch. Also, and this bit of wisdom is gratis, never take a hair recommendation from a stand-up comic. And, on top of these two bits of advice, never fall asleep while someone is in the vicinity of your head with a pair of scissors and/or bottles of chemicals.

After two weeks of one-night stands in fourteen different cities, I ended up in Pittsburgh for a week and had gone into Chez Butch upon the recommendation of Pam Foley, a stand-up who never has liked me much. Two weeks of strange water and shampoo donated by bad hotels had done even more damage than usual to my shoulder-length, overly permed, overly colored, red hair. I needed help. What I got was hair no longer than one inch all over my head dyed the color of anemic doo-doo.

That night, to go onstage, I'd donned a burnt-orange UT baseball cap to cover the mess that was my head. This clashed terribly with the only clean outfit I had left—a pink-and-green mid-calf housedress over lime-green leggings and my pink lace-up high-tops. Luckily, looking funny is not a drawback in my chosen profession.

Now I stood in front of the hotel dresser mirror, my hair, what was left of it, newly washed and standing up in strange little spikes all over my head. Being naked didn't help. I was pulling on my UT football jersey and slipping my feet into my Bullwinkle bedroom slippers when the phone rang. It was 1:30 A.M. Pittsburgh time, 12:30 A.M. Austin, Texas, time. I picked up the phone, knowing it was my friend Phoebe.

"You won't believe my hair," I said by way of greeting.

"I could give about your hair. Kimmey, you have a serious amount of phone calls," Phoebe said.

"Who?"

"Who not? Pucci called, of course. I think I talk to that man more than you ever do."

"What'd he want?" I asked, settling down into the lifeless pillows that came with the lifeless hotel room. Pucci was Detective Sal Pucci of the Chicago Police Department. We'd met a while back when a former boyfriend of mine—okay, a former one-night stand—decided to die on me. And I mean that literally. Pucci was everything I didn't particularly like in a man: small, dark, aggressive, and smart-mouthed. He was also extremely sexy—a trait he was more than willing to prove to me anytime anywhere. I'd opted just to wonder about that particular charm. So far.

Phoebe said, "He wanted to know where you were, how

you were, and if you were sleeping with anyone significant."

"God, he's such an asshole."

"I mentioned that," Phoebe said.

"Who else?"

"This is where it gets strange."

"Don't talk about strange until you see my hair."

"The Cajun connection has reared its ugly head."

I hate it when Phoebe talks cryptic. Especially when I'm having a bad hair eon. "Slowly and succinctly, please," I urged.

"Your cousin Norvella called."

"You're kidding."

"Your cousin Barbara Sue called."

"Jesus."

"And, your, excuse the expression, me-maw called."

"Oh, shit, what's going on?"

"It seems," Phoebe said, great disdain tainting her voice, "that your, excuse the expression, paw-paw has injured himself. He's in the hospital."

I sat up in bed, my heart in my throat. This was bad. If I was getting calls from cousins, this was definitely bad. "Is he dead?" I asked.

"No," Phoebe said. "He broke his leg when he fell out of his pirogue while seining for crab. Does this make sense?"

I fell back on the pillows and let out a sigh of relief. "Yes," I sighed. "Well, I'm glad that's all it is—"

"But wait! There's more," Phoebe said, doing her Ronco announcer voice.

"Can I handle this?" I asked.

"Probably not. As you know, your parents are somewhere in the Antarctic doing their cute little 'we're old but we're spunky' tour, and it seems that, according to Cousin Norvella and Cousin Barbara Sue, it's your mother's turn to watch, excuse the expression, Paw-Paw, so, as your mother is off freezing her buns somewhere exotic, it falls to you, according to Cousin Norvella and Cousin Barbara Sue, to come to the rescue of, excuse the expression, Paw-Paw."

"What?"

"Do you really want me to repeat that sentence?" Phoebe asked.

"No. Actually, I want you never to have uttered that sentence."

We were both silent for a while. Finally, I said, "Is there any way you didn't find me?"

"No way in hell."

"Phoebe!"

"Call your, excuse the expression, me-maw and let me get some sleep."

With that she hung up, leaving me alone and feeling unloved. Knowing my me-maw, she was sitting by the phone waiting for me to call, and had been since Paw-Paw broke his leg; I picked up the phone and dialed.

"Me? I'm not gonna deal with that man, Kimberly. That man break his leg, that his problem, yeah?" Me-Maw said. "Your mama s'pose to take care him, yeah? Not me! I done throwed that man out thirty-five year ago and I ain't takin' care for him no way!"

"Me-Maw, I'm supposed to be on TV tomorrow," I reasoned. And it was true. It was local cable access, but it was, by God, TV.

"Oo-eee! Oo-eee!" Me-Maw yelled. "You be on Johnny?"

"Johnny's not on anymore, Me-Maw."

"Whatever. That new guy, yeah? You gonna be on wid him?"

"No, actually, it's a local show here in Pittsburgh, Me-Maw, but that's not the point—"

4

"Don't you tell me 'bout no point, girl," Me-Maw said sternly. "That man laying in the hospital wid his leg broke, you don't tell me 'bout no point. Norvella and Barbara Sue say they ain't takin' care him again and Betsy ain't got the room her house. You aunts is all too onry and they got a mad-on wid your paw-paw and you know them boy cousins of yours married women don't know nothing 'bout carin' for they kin, so, girl, you gotta come down to Port Arthur and take care of you paw-paw, and that's all there is to it, you hear?"

"How long is he going to be in the hospital?" I asked, resigned.

"They let him go tomorrow in the morning. You be there in the morning, yeah?"

"Me-Maw, I've got that show—"

"Oo-eee, girl. TV mean more to you than you own paw-paw?"

"Me-Maw—"

"You jest gonna leave him sit in the hospiddle waitin' room for a day or two, yeah?"

"Me-Maw—"

"Well, I jest hope that leg don't swell up so much they gotta cut it off, yeah?"

"I'll take the first plane out of here in the morning," I said.

"That's a good girl," Me-Maw said. "But that man can rot for all I care. Oo-eee, that's the trute!"

I took a flight from Pittsburgh to Atlanta, from Atlanta to Houston, and from Houston I got a puddle jumper to Port Arthur, Texas. And all the while all I could think of was Paw-Paw. He was my family connection. The only one in a long line on two sides who resembled me in the slightest.

My father is six feet, five inches tall and weighs two

hundred and eighty pounds. He went to SMU on a football scholarship back in the early sixties, and he met my mother at a restaurant in Dallas where she was modeling lingerie for the mostly male lunchtime crowd. My mother is six feet one and still weighs what she did then: one hundred and twenty-five pounds. My grandmother, Me-Maw, is six feet even. My mother's sisters, all seven of them, range in height from five feet nine to six feet two. Next to me, Cousin Norvella is the runt of the litter, coming in at barely five feet seven.

And then there's Paw-Paw, from whom I received my midget gene. At five feet and one-half inch, he has weighed no more than one hundred and fifteen pounds at any time in his entire eighty-two years. We've always had a special relationship, he and I. Secretly, I believed he always loved me best because I'm the only person he's taller than—by one-half inch. It may be a strange bond, but it's our bond.

My grandparents have been separated since long before my birth. Actually, Me-Maw allowed him to stay in the house until the last of her eight children, my mother, had left the nest. The next day, she threw all his belongings into the ditch that runs in front of the house and told him, in essence, never to darken her door again.

As I recall the story, Paw-Paw, at that time, drank like a fish and chewed tobacco. He gave up drinking immediately, but Me-Maw refused to take him back. So he gave up chewing. She still refused to take him back. Being a true Cajun woman, Me-Maw was, and still is, a clean freak. Having a man in the house seemed to dirty the place up automatically. With Paw-Paw gone, the house shone. She liked that.

They have not, of course, divorced, because good Cajun Catholics don't do that. Over the years, Paw-Paw has attempted to woo her back, but to no avail. A good man may be hard to find, but even a good one isn't worth a dirty house.

I got off the puddle jumper, deplaning (the attendant actually said that, "Be careful as you deplane," I swear to you!) onto the tarmac at Jefferson County Airport, and felt the full weight of summer in Port Arthur, Texas, hit me.

The emissions from all the refineries hazed the sky, allowing the sun no more than a weak peek at us mortal souls. That, however, did not stop the power of its heat. Radiating off the tarmac, the temperature had to be over one hundred degrees, and the humidity more than two hundred percent, if that's possible. There wasn't a breath of air, other than the artificial breeze created by the engine exhaust of the planes, and the stench was unbearable: exhaust fumes mixed with the cabbage-fart smell of one refinery, mixed with the sulfur smell of another, mixed with other unidentifiable smells. Some people think of their grandma's house and remember smells of cookies baking, hot chocolate, apple cider. I think of my grandmother and remember smells of dead fish and cabbage farts. Ah, memories!

I mentally held my nose and walked to the doors that led into the airport waiting room. Cousin Norvella was waiting for me. Norvella, as I said, is five feet, seven inches tall. I didn't mention she weighs two hundred pounds, or that she never heard the expression "fat and jolly." She had a two-year-old hanging on to one leg and a snotty-nosed infant on one hip. Two boys between the ages of three and five were running through the waiting room, jumping on passengers' laps and knocking over briefcases. Norvella would occasionally look over her shoulder and yell, in a high, fingernails-on-blackboard kind of voice, "Stop that!" They, of course, wouldn't stop and she, of course, didn't really care. Form for form's sake.

As I came in the door she leaned down and hugged me, the infant falling toward me, gumming my shoulder, and wiping its filthy nose on my shirt. "Well, you got here!"

Norvella said. "Your hair looks awful!" (This from the hair-spray queen of the greater Beaumont/Port Arthur/Orange metropolitan region.) "Trevor, Dustin! You boys get over here and meet your cousin Kimberly Anne!"

"How's Paw-Paw?" I asked.

"Holding his own. They're gonna keep him in the hospital another day or two."

"What!?!"

She widened her eyes at my exclamation.

"Me-Maw said they were throwing him out today and I had to get here immediately," I said.

She grabbed the two older boys by the scruff of the neck, dragging them off the lap of a hapless traveler, and said, "Oh, you know Me-Maw. She tends to exaggerate."

"I had a TV gig!"

Norvella's eyes got big. "Johnny Carson?"

Norvella drove me straight to Me-Maw's house, passing rice fields dotted with feeding blackbirds and flat pastures with resident grazing cows. We took the Port Arthur Beaumont Highway, passing the Babe Didrikson Zaharias Memorial Golf Course (women do well when they leave Port Arthur—case in point, Ms. Zaharias and Janis Joplin), passing through part of Port Arthur, close to the refineries, then we took the cutoff to the Groves, where my grandmother and most of my kinfolk lived.

Norvella spent the better part of the drive leaning over into the back seat to slap at one child or another. Since no one but the infant was buckled in, it was a difficult feat to achieve. We did a lot of weaving from one lane to another and jumped an occasional curb.

We pulled into Me-Maw's, Norvella miraculously managing to keep the car on the barely wide enough for an American car driveway and out of the six-foot-deep ditch on either side of it. The small white frame house had changed little since my last visit five years before. The pecan trees in the front yard were still whitewashed halfway up, the grass was still cut shorter than my current hair, there were still exactly two geraniums each in two pots on either side of the three steps leading up to the front door. The front door had been freshly painted red, but of course I cannot remember the front door of Me-Maw's house ever not being freshly painted red.

As we got my luggage out of the car, Me-Maw came bursting out of the front door, her large arms open wide, yelling, "Oo-eee! My great-grandbabies!" and grabbed Norvella's little rug rats to her ample bosom. I, of course, got the bosom treatment but a moment later. "Oo-eee! My littlest grandbaby! Kimberly, what happened to you hair?"

The inside of the house had changed little over the years. I thought that possibly the Early American couch was new, but it looked almost exactly like every other Early American couch Me-Maw had ever owned, and I think the number was now reaching epic proportions. Everything was spotless and exact, down to the rows of knickknacks on the knickknack shelves, each dusted daily and all aligned within an inch of their lives. The picture of Jesus was centered over the Early American couch, a crucifix hung over the La-Z-Boy recliner. In the kitchen, a depiction of the Last Supper hung behind the chrome-and-Formica dinette set. Me-Maw's collection of Depression-ware sugar bowls lined a windowsill, while the other windowsill boasted her collection of toaster covers—everything from a knitted cover which was actually a doll's skirt to a hen under whose ample feathers rested a toaster, not an egg.

"We gonna have a family reunion tommorow over to Sabine Park, so I glad you got here early," Me-Maw said, pouring me my fourth cup of heavy, dark, burned-smelling coffee. I wasn't sure how much more of this stuff the aloe-vera plant sitting next to me at her kitchen table was going to be able to take.

"Me-Maw," I said sternly, "you said Paw-Paw was getting out of the hospital today, and I gave up a TV gig—"

"You a good girl, Kimberly Anne," she said, patting me on the head. "You paw-paw don't deserve such a good girl, no."

"But Me-Maw, you said he was getting out of the hospital today, so I—"

"I got some crawfish *etouffee* in here," Me-Maw said, opening the refrigerator. "I heat it up in the microwave, it good as new, you love it, yeah?"

"Me-Maw—"

"I tell you 'bout Mrs. DuPres over to Nederland?" she said, dumping the crawfish *etouffee* in a microwave dish and sticking it in. "Cancer!" she said in a stage whisper. "Et up most her womanly organs. They operate for like twelve hour—don't do no good. Cut out most her woman stuff and half her stomach." She leaned over and whispered, "Limp nodes." Straightening up, she said, "That cancer get them limp nodes, you best cross youself and call the priest 'cause it all over but the shoutin', yeah?"

"Me-Maw, I don't know Mrs. DuPres—"

"Sho you do, yeah? Mrs. DuPres? Lottie DuPres? She Linda DuPres' mama, what married Lonnie Earl Hebert. You remember Linda DuPres?"

"No, Me-Maw, I don't know that many people—"

"Well, Linda DuPres and Lonnie Earl Hebert, they go to school wid you mama—or was it you Aunt Sylvia? Anyway, Lottie DuPres had twelve chilren." Me-Maw, who had eight, went "tsk, tsk." She shook her head. "You cain't 'spect to have no twelve babies and not have your woman stuff go bad, yeah?"

"Well, it would seem to put a strain—"

"Oo-eee, that ain't nothin' to wad happen to Rose Theriot what married Antoine Theriot's boy Ronnie, yeah? She got twins and her womb dropped right out! *Non menti!*" (Loosely translated, "I'm lying, I'm dying.")

"Me-Maw—"

"Tomorrow you see all the kinfolk ain't seen you since you was little bitty thing!" She took the crawfish *etouffee* out of the microwave and set the steamy plate in front of me, then looked at me, her face getting stern. "You hair really bad, Kimberly. Who you let do that to you, girl?"

"Well—"

"I get you my wig, yeah? That look good, *te parartre!*" (Loosely translated, "You bet your shiny heinie!")

🐾 I spent the rest of the afternoon doing duty stuff. I borrowed Me-Maw's Chevy and drove to the hospital but wasn't able to see Paw-Paw, as he was sleeping. Getting back to the house, I was greeted by three aunts, four female cousins, and my grandmother, all with assorted wigs. It was the consensus of everyone present that the Louisiana branch of the family would probably never again speak to the Port Arthur branch of the family if I and my real hair showed up at the family reunion. I selected an early Tammy Wynette number, thanked them profusely, ate the dinner forced on me—fried oysters, fried shrimp, barbecued crab, "dirty rice," and a big bowl of chicken gumbo—and went to bed in a room that hadn't had a window opened in it in twenty-five years. There I slept the sleep of the bad-haired but sufficiently stuffed.

Chapter

2

I woke up the next morning with my grandmother dribbling water in my face. A quaint family custom. "Oo-eee, they's a boy on the phone for Kimberly!"

"Wha?"

"The phone! A boy! You want I should tell him you busy, yeah?" Me-Maw said and giggled.

"I'll get it," I said, sliding out of the bed and heading into the hall to the only phone in the house. I picked it up and said, "Hello?"

"Hey, Kruse," Pucci said. "Who was that woman?"

"That was no woman, that was my grandmother."

"No shit? Sounded too ethnic to be the WASP princess's grandmother."

"Cute. What do you want? Why did you call? And who gave you this number?"

For a while, back in Chicago, Detective Pucci thought I had caused the death of my former friend. For some reason, though, even thinking of me as a possible murderer didn't stop him from propositioning me on a daily, if not hourly, basis. We became friends, after a fashion, and talked periodically long distance. But as Phoebe pointed out, with me being on the road as much as I am, he talks to her more often than to me. In my worst nightmare I see Pucci coming to Austin to find me—finding Phoebe instead, the two of them falling madly in love, and Pucci becoming my blood brother-in-law. In a nightmare only slightly less awful, I see myself in a roomful of Italian in-laws, with snot-nosed brats resembling Cousin Norvella's, awaiting word of my husband Pucci's condition after his shoot-out with armed baddies. Basically, with nightmares like these, I try not to dream about Pucci at all.

"Some way to greet a friend and almost lover," Pucci said.

"In your dreams," I said.

"Always," he said.

I've got to admit the guy does have a way about him. "What do you want, Pucci?" I asked, getting back to business. "It's early and I haven't even had my morning pee, much less my morning coffee."

"Don't try to arouse me now, Kruse. You had your chance."

I pulled up a chair and sat down. "Is this really the way you want to spend your morning?" I asked.

"Any morning spent with you, my sweet—"

"What do you want?"

He sighed. "Well, I can see we're in a foul mood. Here I call long distance just to find out how your grandfather is—"

"How did you know I had a grandfather and that his condition was of concern, huh, Pucci?"

"Phoebe told me."

"Well, isn't that nice."

"What's that supposed to mean?"

"Absolutely nothing," I said, my voice tight. "It just seems you and Phoebe are getting fairly close for two people who've never even met."

"Who says we haven't met?" Pucci said.

I stood up from the chair. "What?"

"Of course we haven't met," Pucci said. "How could we have? How's your grandfather?"

"Fine," I said.

"That's great." Pucci laughed, a throaty thing that had been known to arouse certain baser instincts in yours truly. "God, I love it when you get jealous."

"I am not jealous!"

"Look, sweetheart, honey, doll, I gotta go now. Murders to solve and all that shit. But listen, I'll keep in touch, and if I can't find you, well, I'll just call Pheobe—"

I hung up and went to the bathroom.

☙ I called Paw-Paw and found out he was doing okay, was delighted to hear from me, was looking forward to spending time with me, couldn't wait to get out of the hospital, and had I learned to cook Cajun yet? After that I put on my Tammy Wynette wig, a pair of my newest jeans, some un-alarming white sneakers, and my Hard Rock Cafe T-shirt, the only clothes I had with me—okay, the only clothes I owned—appropriate for a family reunion with the Cajun side of the family. (My father's family, being liberals, pretend to tolerate my clothing.)

Then I helped Me-Maw pack up the food for the reunion, which took up all the trunk and half the back seat of her standard-sized Chevy. Me-Maw's sister Adele, a widow, was riding with us (in the front seat—I, as a grandchild, got the small portion of the back that was left). The immediate branch of the Port Arthur clan (my grandmother and her two sisters living in Port Arthur, all their children, all their children's children, and their children's children's children) met at the K-Mart parking lot to caravan to the park on Sabine Lake.

At the beginning of the trip, Me-Maw and Adele talked the entire time, Me-Maw turning around in her seat to make sure I heard and responded properly, her hands off the wheel more than on whenever she spoke, in true Cajun fashion. (My father and I have always found watching my mother talk on the phone a source of great amusement—her hands are flying, stabbing the air for emphasis, describing lengths and sizes, and generally going faster than her mouth.)

Some of the larger trucks and many of the cars on the other side of the road did not appreciate Me-Maw's style of travel, but she didn't seem to notice.

The closer we got to Sabine Lake, however, the quieter both old women got.

I tried some endless prattle of my own, but got no response from the front seat. Finally, knowing it was not my grandmother's nor my Aunt Adele's way to be quiet for more than twenty seconds at a time, I asked, "Is something wrong?"

Me-Maw glanced at me through the rearview mirror. "*Oui?*"

"You're both just so quiet," I said.

The two old ladies looked at each other and Me-Maw shook her head. Aunt Adele turned slightly around in her seat. "It jest that we gonna see somebody today we ain't spoke to in close to forty-five year. Somebody we, well, had a mad-on with."

"Oh?" I said, ready for a good story. I was greeted instead by Aunt Adele's back and silence. Finally, I said, "Who?"

Me-Maw glanced at me again in the mirror. "Our cousin

Leticia. Our mama and Leticia's mama was sisters. Me and Leticia was in the same grade together, and we was close like sisters, yeah, Adele?"

Adele nodded her head. "Yeah, that the truth."

Again both women were silent. I waited for what seemed an eternity, finally interested in something the two old ladies had to say, but they weren't exactly forthcoming. Unable to contain myself, I said, "So why haven't you seen her in forty-five years?"

The two shared a glance again, then Me-Maw sighed. "Leticia, she don't marry so well."

"Oh?" I inquired.

Adele said, "She marry a bad man, a black Cajun."

Then I got it. Forty-five years ago a relative of mine had married into another race and my old-fashioned, bigoted family couldn't handle it. That made sense.

"Well," I said, tolerance personified, "in this day and age, interracial marriage is no biggie. I hope the two of you have learned to be a little more understanding in the last forty-five years."

Me-Maw and Aunt Adele looked at each other again, but this time the look was not secretive, but puzzled.

"What she goin' on about?" Aunt Adele asked Me-Maw.

"I be dipped if I know," Me-Maw answered. Turning around in her seat to look at me, she said, "What you be talkin' about, girl?"

"About Cousin Leticia marrying a black man—"

Both old women hooted with laughter. Aunt Adele said, "I didn't say black man—I say bad man—"

"You said black Cajun—"

"Genevieve," Aunt Adele said, "she don' know from black Cajun?"

Me-Maw sighed. "That girl don' know nothin'." She turned

around in her seat again. "Kimberly Anne, that's like . . . black Irish—you heard about that?"

"Ah, yeah—"

"Black Cajun is got black hair, pale skin, and mostly blue eyes, yeah, Adele?"

"Good-lookin' peoples, them black Cajuns. But half the time they no good." She looked sideways at Me-Maw. "Comes from being too *jolle,* yeah, Genevieve?"

Me-Maw smiled. "We lucky in this family we all so damn ugly."

Aunt Adele smiled back and lightly touched Me-Maw's hand where it rested on the steering wheel.

"Well," I said, "I still don't understand why you haven't spoken in forty-five years."

Me-Maw shook her head. "It a long story, Kimberly Anne. Not for chilren ears." She sighed. "But we see her today, yeah, Adele?"

"That right, Genevieve, we gonna see Leticia today."

We pulled into a parking area by a large pavilion on a cove of Sabine Lake. Willow and ash trees grew along the banks of the lake, with an occasional large pecan tree in the park for shade. Clumps of dead trees stood sentinel in the water of Sabine Lake. There had to be a hundred cars in the lot and it looked like most of them were there for the Foret (pronounced "Fo-ray") family reunion.

We parked and got out and the three of us started unloading the car. The other aunts, great-aunts, and cousins came before and after us, parking their cars and unloading the food. I helped Me-Maw and Aunt Adele carry our stuff to the tables lined up under the pavilion. I'd never seen so much food. Or so much Saran Wrap. Down a slope toward the cove, men in comical chef's hats and "funny" aprons were busy over cookstoves, some with large pots on top of them.

Then the introductions began. I met more cousins, second, third, and removed, than a person has a right to have, then in-laws, soon-to-bes, and even a couple of out-laws ("My brother Jackie's married to your cousin Ramona's sister-in-law, yeah?")

Then I heard a voice I recognized behind me say, "Kimberly Anne, is that you?" A deep, sexy voice that always reminded me of the actress Suzanne Pleshette. My favorite cousin—Barbara Sue.

During my annual summer visit to Port Arthur, when I was in grammar school and Barbara Sue was in high school, I thought she was the coolest person who ever lived. She smoked floral-patterned cigarettes and taught me the appropriate obscene gesture for just about any occasion. She was the only one of the Port Arthur cousins to make it to college—although she only lasted two semesters before flunking out.

I remember perching on the footboard of her bed, listening to Mick Jagger sing "Beast of Burden" on her little bedroom stereo. Every time Mick's voice would go low on the word "burden," Barbara Sue would shout, "Righteous!" make an obscene gesture, and fall backward onto the bed. I'd follow suit, mimicking her every word and deed.

In junior high, when I first met my friend Phoebe, the only truly cool thing I brought to the relationship was my vast assortment of obscene gestures learned at the knee of Cousin Barbara Sue.

I hadn't seen Barbara Sue in fifteen years. After her two not so productive semesters of college, she'd run off with some guy. I later heard from my mother, who'd heard from her mother, that Barbara Sue had straightened up and married well.

I turned to see my way cool cousin. And couldn't find her. Instead I saw a woman in her mid-thirties, dressed in a mid-calf-length, ruffled Swiss-dotted dress, with a rounded collar covered in ruffles and floppy short, ruffled sleeves. On her head was a wide-brimmed flowered hat covering bleached, permed blond hair and shading a face wearing so much makeup it was hard to see the person I once knew.

"Barbara Sue?" I asked.

She leaned down and made a kissy noise somewhere near my left cheek, her hands, with their long, pearly-pink fingernails, resting lightly on my shoulders. "Honey, it's so good to see you," she said, the throaty voice an octave higher than it used to be. "I want you to meet my family."

Standing next to her was a man about two inches shorter than she, portly, somewhere in his mid-to-late-forties, wearing a white-on-white summer shirt, square tail out, over khaki pants. His handshake was professional.

"This is my husband, the Reverend Jimmy Lynn Blanton. And these are our children."

The little boy was about twelve, with conservatively cut blond hair, wearing long pants and a white Oxford cloth shirt. The little girl, about seven, was wearing an exact replica of her mother's dress. "This," Barbara Sue said, putting a manicured hand on the head of the boy, "is Matthew Luke, and this"—the hand moved to the ringleted and behatted head of her daughter—"is Naomi Ruth. Say hello to Cousin Kimberly Anne, children."

Both children said "Hello" in unison.

I smiled at the kids and said "Hi" back. "Well, Barbara Sue."

She put her arm around my shoulder and pulled me slightly away from her family. "Now, Kimberly Anne, my mother tells me you've been working in nightclubs, is that right?"

I stiffened. "I'm a comedian. I perform in comedy clubs, usually at night."

She took her arm off me and leaned forward, looking directly into my eyes. "Honey, I just think you should be terribly careful in places like that. I'm not judging you, honey, but nightclubs are where the Devil likes to hang out, tempting people with all flavors of sin." She smiled at me. "You are precious in the eyes of the Lord, Kimberly Anne, and we want to make sure you stay that way."

Jimmy Lynn walked up to join us, the children not far behind. He smiled, exposing a mouthful of expertly capped white teeth. "Kimberly Anne, the Lord gave you a special gift," he said, touching me lightly on the shoulder, "the gift of laughter. It's wonderful you share this gift. Why, Barbara Sue and I were watching a Bob Hope Special on TV just the other night and we both just laughed and laughed." He laughed. "Didn't we, Barbara Sue?"

Barbara Sue laughed. "Just laughed and laughed," she echoed.

"Laughter is good medicine, Kimberly Anne, and should be spread judiciously." His smile wavered, his face working itself into a concerned frown. "But those places! Praise Jesus, Kimberly Anne, we pray for you nightly, we want you to know that. Barbara Sue and I pray for your soul being in those kinds of places."

I started backing up. I couldn't help it. Jimmy Lynn was definitely in my space and Barbara Sue was moving in on my right. The children flanked me on the left. I was being "love-bombed."

"We want you to come visit with us at our church while you're here," Barbara Sue said.

"What church is that?" I asked.

"The Church of the Redeeming Saviour Lord God Jehovah," Jimmy Lynn said. "We're independent Charismatic Baptists."

"How nice," I said, moving backward as quickly as I could. "I think I hear Me-Maw calling me."

I turned and saw Me-Maw and Aunt Adele under the food awning and waved quickly at Barbara Sue and family and fled. I grabbed Me-Maw's large arm. "What happened to Barbara Sue?" I wailed.

"Oh, you met Jimmy Lynn, yeah?" Me-Maw said, smiling. "Don't he look a lot like that Reverend Swaggart in Baton Rouge?"

"Same hairdo," I managed.

"Don' mine them none, girl," Aunt Adele said. "They been trying to get me and you me-maw over to their church for ten year or more, ain't that right, Genevieve?"

"I'm Catholic," Me-Maw said. End of discussion.

Me-Maw glanced up from her food preparations and got very still. I looked where she was looking and saw a tall, thin woman with improbable red hair (much like my own late lamented) wearing a red dress and carrying a blue handbag. Adele glanced up too. "Well, I'll be," she whispered. She looked at Me-Maw. "Genevieve?"

Me-Maw moved around the table and walked out of the shade of the awning. The woman in the red dress saw her. Both stood still for a moment, just looking at each other. Then they ran to each other, their arms around the other, sobbing loudly, Cajun endearments filling the air. Aunt Adele cried quietly beside me and I put my arm around her waist, as it wouldn't comfortably fit her shoulder. "Go on," I said. "Go see Cousin Leticia."

She nodded her head and moved toward the two old women, soon joining the embrace. I felt like crying myself, and I didn't even know what hatchet was being buried.

Me-Maw waved me over. "This here my youngest grand-baby, Kimberly Anne. She Katherine's only child."

"What married that professor fellow?" Leticia said in a singsong voice.

"That's da one," Me-Maw said proudly. In his presence, Me-Maw acted as if my father didn't exist. But around relatives, Me-Maw always managed to mention the fact that he was a full professor at the University of Texas English Department and was referred to as "Dr. Kruse." That Leticia knew what was going on in Me-Maw's family and Me-Maw in hers was not surprising, even though they hadn't spoken in forty-five years. Whatever had gone on between them hadn't shut up other members of the family.

Cousin Leticia hugged me to her skinny bosom. "Well, you little bitty, like your granddaddy—"

"Don' talk 'bout that man—he broke his leg, did you hear that? Crabbing at his age!" Me-Maw went "tsk, tsk."

Cousin Leticia held out her hand. "Willard, honey, you come over here. You meet my cousin Genevieve's baby granddaughter, yeah?" Cousin Leticia beamed. "Kimberly Anne, this my boy Willard."

I turned as Cousin Willard came over. And I was struck dumb. About thirty-five, approximately six feet, two inches tall, he was slender, with what appeared to be good, if not excellent, if not down-right exceptional, upper-body strength. His hair was so black it shone almost blue in the sun. His skin was pale and flawlessly smooth, and his eyes were bluer than any I'd ever encountered. When he smiled (a great, a breathtaking, an unbelievable smile), I could see that his teeth were straight and his cheeks dimpled. He was, quite simply, the best-looking specimen of male hunkitude I'd ever personally encountered.

He held out his hand to me. "Will," he said.

I took his hand and felt electricity shoot through my arm,

pass my heart, and head straight to my womanly organs, so to speak. "Will what?" I asked.

He smiled. I got wet. "My friends call me Will," he said.

I smiled. "My friends call me Kimmey," I said.

He turned to his mother and my grandmother, both beaming at us. "Ma, if you and Cousin Genevieve don't mind, I'll show Kimmey around."

"That be nice," Me-Maw said. "Thank you kindly, Willard. And it was nice finally meeting you."

"Willard a good boy," Cousin Leticia said to Me-Maw as we walked off.

"Spitting image of his daddy," Aunt Adele said in a half-whisper.

Will had his hand lightly on my back, guiding me through the throng of relatives. I could feel the heat from the palm of his hand through the T-shirt and had an incredibly hard time not jumping on him right there. I couldn't remember ever having had such a strong reaction to a man in so short a time, and couldn't help wondering what his reaction was to me. I restrained myself from asking, "Cousin Will, do you want to rip my clothes off as badly as I want to rip off yours?" and followed him toward a dock jutting out into the cove. We went to the end and sat, taking off our shoes and dangling our feet in the tepid, greenish, murky water of Sabine Lake. It was about then I remembered the Tammy Wynette wig sitting on top of my head, and the ugly reason it was there.

One day I'll teach a class, "How to Attract Men 101." Lesson Number One: Try to have hair. Preferably your own.

Chapter 3

THE SUMMER MONTHS ON THE TEXAS GULF COAST CONSIST OF high temperatures, higher humidity, and mosquitoes the size of mid-sized Japanese cars. As it was now mid-July, the temperature at eleven-thirty in the morning was ninety-three degrees, the humidity was one hundred and fifty, and the mosquitoes on the lake were parched. And I was their drinking fountain. The heat and humidity caused me to sweat, particularly my head, which loosened the wig and made it itch. Every time I scratched, the wig would move.

I suppose it was at a somewhat crazy angle, without my knowledge, when Cousin Will said, "Why are you wearing that thing?"

I sighed, took it off, and shoved it in my lap. "Bad haircut, huh?" he said, reaching up and smoothing my hair down. The heat, humidity, and mosquitoes all went away. I was on a tropical island, by a clear blue stream, and it was my duty as the concubine of the island emperor to seduce the lovely white man before me . . .

"Me-Maw was embarrassed about my hair."

Will laughed. "She'll live. Actually"—he touched my hair again—"it looks better than that silly wig."

"That wig must have looked bad," I said, smiling up at the dimples.

"How come no one ever told me I had such a wonderful cousin?" he said, his voice quiet.

I put my hands between my knees to keep from grabbing at his belt buckle. "Well, I have to admit no one ever told me about you, either."

"This is the first time we've been to one of the family reunions. Ma and the rest of the family had a falling-out about something," he said, touching my bare arm.

"My family and I rarely come because we live in Austin," I said.

"I'm glad you came this time," he said.

"Me too," I said.

He would have kissed me at that moment (I swear to you) if Cousin Norvella's high screeching voice hadn't cut through our reverie.

"Kimberly Anne!" I turned to see her, and what a sight it was. She was wearing polyester denim-printed pants and a craft T-shirt resplendent with deflated balloons, satin-ribbon bows, and hand-painted butterflies; the kind of shirt that screams, "Say one word and I'll make you one just like it!"

She was chasing one of her boys, who was chasing a girl about seven, who was screaming and throwing clumps of dirt and weeds. "Dustin! Michelle!" Norvella shouted. "Y'all stop that! Kimberly Anne, Me-Maw wants you—Dustin, put down that dog turd, do you hear me!"

Will got gracefully to his feet and pulled me up. Norvella

hurried over, untying a red bandanna from around her neck. "Well, for Gawd's sake, at least put this over that mess! Michelle Marie! Get off Dustin's head!"

I took the bandanna and put it around my hair, tying it in the back. "How do I look?" I asked Will.

He grinned. "Like an incredibly sexy pirate."

I took that as a compliment and walked with Cousin Norvella back to the pavilion, trying to figure out just how related I was to that incredible hunk of a man.

"So, Norvella," I asked, "Will's our what—third cousin? Fourth?"

She nodded. "Something like that. You see Me-Maw finally talking to Cousin Leticia?"

"Um-hum," I said. "I saw that. What happened anyway?"

Norvella shrugged. "I don't know," she said, her fingernail-on-a-blackboard voice rubbing my nerve endings raw. "Mama said that Willard's daddy was a rotten one, though. Used to beat Leticia up. Left her when she was pregnant with Willard." She went "tsk, tsk." An unfortunate family trait I hoped I'd never inherit. "Then he'd come back ever so often, whenever Leticia had any money—ain't that just the way with men? X-ray vision when it comes to a woman having a little money on her. James Earl can sniff a dime in my purse from across the room, I swear to God! Then Armand—"

"Who?"

She looked at me as if I wasn't quite all there. "Willard's daddy," she said patiently. "Anyway, Armand come back when Willard was in college and tried beating Leticia up again, but Willard was big enough then and beat the crap out of his own daddy." She looked at me. "You believe that?"

"Well, if he was defending his mother—"

"Anyway, that's the last anybody ever heard of old Armand, Mama says. You like my T-shirt?"

Platters of boiled crawfish and boiled shrimp with red sauce and white sauce for dipping, barbecued crab, fried oysters, shrimp bisque, pots of dirty rice, red beans and rice, four different kinds of gumbo (chicken, shrimp, chicken-and-shrimp, and crab with okra), five different kinds of potato salad, four different macaroni salads, three different bean salads, red *boudin* and white *boudin,* sausages of all links and varieties, a pot of shrimp *etouffee,* and all this was only the main table. The dessert table left me stupefied. For my size, I am a rather magnificent eater. I've been known to eat my own weight with very little difficulty. Needless to say, with the exception of Cousin Will, this spread was the highlight of my month.

Then I found out that good Cajun women don't eat. That is to say, not until all the menfolk and children have been thoroughly fed. I'm small, but I'm also twenty-nine years old and was known by some of those present. I couldn't sneak into the children's line. No matter how hard I tried.

We stood behind the tables, Me-Maw, Aunt Adele, Cousin Leticia and I, and watched other people grab up all the good food. Occasionally we would help someone to a little more, lest he go hungry. I sipped a styrofoam cup of Diet Coke that Me-Maw had handed me from the large communal bottles of soda in the ice chest under the table and thought nasty thoughts about my male relatives and their offspring. Me-Maw sipped from her cup of RC Cola, Aunt Adele had an iced tea, and Cousin Leticia had a Big Red.

Will passed before our table where we were ladling out red beans and rice, and smiled at me. "I'll save you a place— over by the dock?"

"Sounds great," I said, smiling back.

Me-Maw nudged me in the ribs and she and Aunt Adele made eye contact above me.

" 'And the truth shall set ye free," Cousin Leticia said out of the blue.

"*Qui c'est sa,* Leticia?" Me-Maw said.

"Did I tell you I been born again, Genevieve?" Leticia said. "I found Jesus in my heart and Jesus he set me free."

"Well, that's real nice, yeah?" Me-Maw and Aunt Adele exchanged glances.

"Do you know Jesus as you one true Saviour, Genevieve?" Leticia asked.

Me-Maw drew herself up to her full six feet. "I been goin' mass two time a week ever week my whole life! I know Jesus? *Pooyah-ee!*"

"Jesus say the truth will set you free."

"I know that!" Me-Maw said, getting a little put out about the whole conversation. Me-Maw never liked anyone doubting her faith. Personally, I thought the quote was from Shakespeare, or Thomas Paine, or somebody else rather than Jesus, but now didn't seem the time to make corrections.

"I hear you, Cousin Leticia," said Barbara Sue, slipping up on my blind side. "Praise Jesus."

Leticia looked at Barbara Sue, not a particularly friendly look. "Hello, Barbara Sue. How you be?"

Barbara Sue smiled a gigantic smile and hugged Leticia, who seemed to back up a little as she did so. "Well, I'm just fine, Cousin Leticia. And I'm so glad you're back in the bosom of your family! Praise Jesus!"

Leticia smiled weakly. "Thank you kindly, Barbara Sue." Her smile got a little brighter, and a little mean-looking. "How's your husband, the preacher man?"

The light in Barbara Sue's smile never faded. The wattage, if anything, went up several notches. "The Lord's been good to us, Leticia. Jimmy Lynn's church is doing wonderfully well and the children are just blessed lambs of Christ!"

"Well, that's so nice," Leticia said, weakening again.

Barbara Sue turned her sugar on Me-Maw and Aunt Adele, hugging them and kissing the air next to their faces. "Me-Maw, you're looking wonderfully well today."

"Thank you kindly, Barbara Sue. That's a mighty pretty hat you're wearing."

Barbara Sue touched the brim of her large flowered hat. "Well, how sweet!" She took it off her head and handed it to Me-Maw. "It's yours!" She waved and was off.

Me-Maw stood there with the wide-brimmed flowered hat in her hand. "Oo-eee, what I supposed to do with this ugly thing?"

All three old women, and one young woman, giggled fit to be tied.

"Lord, help me," Cousin Leticia said, looking down the long line of people stuffing their faces.

"*Qui n'a?*" Me-Maw countered.

"Lookee there!" Leticia said, nodding furtively at the only woman in the line of men and children.

"Oo-eee!" Me-Maw said under her breath. "What she do here, yeah?"

"Leticia, don' you even look at her," Aunt Adele said. "Like she not even there, yeah?"

The woman in line got to our red beans and rice and smiled sweetly at Cousin Leticia. The stranger was about ten years or so younger than Me-Maw, Aunt Adele, and Cousin Leticia, somewhere in her mid-to-late sixties. Her hair was dyed a yellow blond and worn ratted into a beehive. The heavy clownish makeup on her face only accentuated the lines etched deep into her skin. She wore bright canary-yellow, skin-tight stretch pants over bulbous thighs and a lime-green accordion-pleated angel top printed with one big flower on the front and one on the back, reaching to about mid-stomach. And stomach there was, believe me. I was reminded strongly of the old woman Cher used to do on "The Sonny and Cher Show."

"Leticia, *comment ca va?*" the woman said, smiling brightly, the teeth so straight and white they could be nothing but false.

"*Sa bien,* Dorisca. I didn't know you was comin'." Leticia said, her voice betraying the fact that she wished the woman dead.

"Oh, I come with my friend Enic." Dorisca put her hand on the shoulder of the man in front of her. "Enic, look and meet my old friend Leticia."

Enic, a small man in his seventies, turned. "Don't go introducing me to my own kin, woman. Leticia she my Aunt Terese's sister-in-law's son's cousin, yeah, Leticia?"

"That right, Enic. How you be?"

He waved his hand. "*Comme se, comme sa,*" he said.

"How you wife be?" Me-Maw asked.

Enic turned red. "She be fine, Genevieve. She be home in Armentine."

The two moved on, with the three old ladies looking daggers after them.

"Nerve!" Aunt Adele said.

"She come here, I don't believe it, no!" Me-Maw said. She turned to Leticia. "You be okay?"

Leticia shuddered. "That hussy."

"You bein' nice, Leticia, I tell you what!" Me-Maw said.

"That whore!" Leticia said.

Me-Maw patted Leticia's shoulder. Leticia shook herself, then yawned and shook her head. "I be tired," she said, obviously ready to forget the unforgettable Dorisca. She stretched and took another sip of her Big Red. "I be up mos' the night making Mississippi mud pie. You like that, girl?" she asked me.

"Sounds great," I said.

"You know Jesus?" she asked me.

"Yes, ma'am," I said.

"Ha!" Me-Maw said. "She Episcopalian!"

All three women turned and looked at me.

"Well, it's practically Catholic," I said under my breath, remembering my father's favorite line: "Episcopalians are Catholics who don't sweat." (My Lutheran daddy and my Catholic mama had decided, upon marriage, to compromise, thereby pissing off both sides of the family.)

Cousin Leticia yawned again.

"Leticia, you go lay down, girl, what wrong wid you, huh?" Me-Maw said.

Leticia shook her head. "Jest tired."

"Go lay down in the car, girl. Go on now, yeah?"

Leticia crumpled her styrofoam cup and put it in the sack under the table. "Oo-eee, I be tired, all righty. I jest go lay down a minute. You come get me when it time for us to eat, yeah?"

"Go now, we get you, yeah?"

Leticia headed for the parking lot and Me-Maw and Aunt Adele started in. "Jesus this and Jesus that! Oo-eee, that girl gettin' strange, yeah?" Aunt Adele said.

"She be goin' one of them churches what talk in tongues, I hear, and I ain't talking *français!*" Me-Maw said.

"You shoulda hear her before you get here, Kimberly Anne," Aunt Adele said. "She say 'I born again' how many time, Genevieve?"

"Too many time, I tell you what!" Me-Maw went "tsk,

tsk." "Getting worse than Barbara Sue, I tell you what! Like we ain't been good Catholics our whole life anyway, yeah?"

"What was all that with that Dorisca woman?" I asked.

Me-Maw and Aunt Adele exchanged looks again over my head. "Well . . ." Me-Maw said.

Aunt Adele leaned down toward me and whispered, "That Dorisca Judice! Leticia's black Cajun runned off with her back in 1958, yeah, Genevieve?"

"And she still messin' with other girls' men, I see," Me-Maw said. She folded her hands over her ample bosom and looked to the table where Dorisca Judice and Enic had sat down.

"I knowed that Enic when we was in school in Armentine," Me-Maw said. "He was stupid then, too."

"He don' think nobody gonna tell Lucia he here with that hussy, no? Half da peoples here kin to Lucia's family one way or the other. He got another think comin', I tell you that!" Aunt Adele said.

The line of men and children was beginning to dwindle, at a rate not quite equal to that of my escalating hunger. "Can we eat now?" I asked.

"Girl, you like a little baby!" Me-Maw said, "tsk-tsking" away. She shooed me with her hand. "Go! Eat!"

Nobody had to tell me twice. I got in line behind two teenaged boys who were related to me in some way, I suppose, and I prayed to anyone listening that they keep their filthy paws off my portion of the grub. I got two plates heaping with food and, with a new Diet Coke under my arm, headed for the dock and Cousin Will.

He was sitting with an older child who greatly resembled one of Cousin Norvella's brats. About twelve, the boy was talking a mile a minute around the food in his mouth, his hands flying as he spoke. He might be four generations out of the bayou, but that hand thing is genetic.

I sat down next to Will, putting him in the middle between the boy and myself. "Hi," I said.

Will looked over and smiled. I was glad I was sitting down, that way I wouldn't have to rely on weak knees to hold me upright. "Welcome," he said. Pointing at the boy, he said, "This is Jesse. He's Cousin Norvella's oldest and he plays Little League and is going to be going out for the junior-high football team in the fall, that right, Jesse?"

At which point Jesse began a dissertation on the relative merits of baseball versus football, basketball versus everything else, and how soccer was for nerds. Then he said, "You're Kimmey, right?"

I nodded.

"You the one who's a comedian, right?"

"Yep."

He grinned, exposing a mouthful of far too many teeth jammed into a space not quite large enough to accommodate half what he had. "I got a joke to tell you."

Inwardly I sighed. I will admit right now that I'm a little defensive about my chosen profession. You know how doctors are always being asked for free advice and lawyers are always being waylaid at parties? Well, comics get told a lot of jokes. I, personally, don't tell jokes. That's not my job. Stand-up comedy is body language, facial expression, and the use and misuse of words. It is not JOKES!

I looked into the beady eyes of the issue of my least favorite cousin and steeled myself to neutrality. "Oh?" I said.

Will glanced my way and smiled. I melted and smiled sweetly at Jesse. "What's that?" I said.

"Okay, listen," Jesse said, his hands waving madly. "Why did King Kong climb the Empire State Building?"

I continued to smile. "I don't know. Why did King Kong climb the Empire State Building?"

It was at this point that Jesse started laughing. "Because . . . he's too . . . big . . . to fit . . . in the elevator!"

I laughed politely. Will laughed politely. We were saved from any more by Cousin Norvella's screech.

"Jesse Marvin Attler! You get your butt over here and help me with your brothers! I mean it now, you hear? Trevor, don't you put that potato salad in the baby's diaper!"

Jesse stood up resigned. "I gotta go," he said.

"Where's your daddy?" I asked, wondering if I've ever actually seen Cousin Norvella's husband.

Jesse snorted. "Huh! Daddy's too smart to come to these things! He's working on somebody's car today, I reckon."

I smiled. "Well, nice meeting you, Jesse."

"Yeah, nice meeting you, too. You don't seem nearly as snotty as Mama said you was."

I blinked. "Why, thank you," I said.

As Jesse got out of earshot, Cousin Will broke into laughter. "He's right, you know," he said. "You aren't as snotty as Norvella thinks you are."

"What did she say?" I demanded. I figured in a fair fight (her with her fists and me with a chair) I could take her.

Will smiled and shook his head. "I haven't the faintest idea. I only met Norvella once when I was fifteen and she was twelve and she cried the entire two hours I was in her company."

I nodded. I remembered Norvella as a child. She cried a lot. About everything.

I'd consumed one plate while Jesse was talking and now started in on the other. This one consisted of a Jell-O ring, fruit salad, and five various desserts, the Mississippi mud pie chief among them. I took a big bite.

"Um," I said, "your mama makes a mean Mississippi mud."

"Yeah, I've really missed that since moving to Port Arthur," Will said. "Though my waistline is grateful."

I perked up. "You live in Port Arthur?"

"Um-hum. I work for Gasco. I'm a petroleum engineer. I was with the plant in Lafyette but I got transferred to the refinery here about a year ago."

"Right here in Port Arthur, huh?" I said.

He smiled. "Yep. Right here."

We looked at each other and I almost forgot about the Mississippi mud pie. Almost.

Then he said, "What's this Jesse was saying about you being a comedian?"

I nodded and tried to talk around a mouthful of chocolate, marshmallow cream, nuts, and other assorted wonders of the world. "Yeah, I do stand-up. Professionally."

He smiled. "No kidding?"

I smiled. "No kidding."

"Okay," he said, rubbing his hands together. "I have a joke for you."

I smiled, while inwardly finding my first fault with this apparently perfect man. "Great!" I said.

"This woman gets her two little boys back, who've been staying with her ex-husband for a few months, and she discovers her ex-husband's filthy mouth has rubbed off. The kids' language is just awful." He looked at me.

"Uh-huh," I said, smiling encouragement.

"So she does just everything she can think of—reward, punishment. Nothing works."

"Uh-huh," I said.

"Finally, she goes to a shrink, explains what she's done to try to cure it and the shrink says, 'Well, I hate to recommend this, but since you've tried everything else, why not try slapping them whenever they say a bad word?' So the woman

35

goes home and the next morning she asks her ten-year-old what he wants for breakfast. He says, 'What ya got?' The woman says, 'I have eggs, cold cereal, or oatmeal.' And the ten-year-old says, 'I'll have some fucking oatmeal.' "

I laughed. He laughed. We both laughed. Will held up his hands. "Wait, I'm not through. So she slaps him. She turns to the seven-year-old and asks him what he wants for breakfast and he says, 'You can bet your ass I don't want any fucking oatmeal!' "

I laughed until my sides hurt. In all fairness to me, he told it really great. Really.

It was about then that the screaming started. I looked up and saw Me-Maw charging across the grass, screaming her lungs out. "*Allons! Allons! Vous-autres!* Willard! Your mama! *Allons!* Call 911! Oo-eee! *Depeche-toi!*"

Will and I jumped up, leaving our plates on the dock, and ran for Me-Maw.

"Cousin Genevieve," Will said, taking Me-Maw's arms. "What's wrong? *Quoi y'a?*"

"Oo-eee! Oo-eee!" Me-Maw said, holding her breasts and gasping for air. "Willard, your mama!" Me-Maw covered her face with her hands and burst into tears.

"Where is she?" Will demanded.

"She went to the car to rest," I told Will and followed him as he ran to the parking lot.

The back door to Cousin Leticia's Buick stood open. She was slumped half in and half out of the car. Her face was swollen almost to the point of being unrecognizable. Her arms and neck were swelling as we watched. Her eyes were swollen closed and she was breathing raggedly. And one lonely and agitated wasp darted about nervously, thrusting himself against the closed windows of the front seat, looking for the hole to freedom.

*   *   *

๛ Will and I waited for Me-Maw to show up with the car at the little clinic in Sabine Pass. Will and I had ridden in the ambulance with Leticia to the clinic, but when Life Flight got there to take her to the larger hospital in Beaumont, we hadn't been able to go. The doctors at the clinic had diagnosed anaphylactic shock, caused by bee or wasp stings, and had called immediately for Life Flight, not having the facilities at the clinic to deal with such a crisis.

We stood in the sun outside the clinic, waiting. I looked around the dreary little town, the flat, empty space that epitomized this end of the Texas Gulf Coast. Me-Maw's Chevy screeched to a halt in front of us.

"She be okay?" Me-Maw asked, sticking her head out her open window.

Will and I rushed to the car, opening the back doors and hopping in. "They've taken her to Beaumont," Will said. "Can you drive me there, Genevieve?"

"You betcha," Me-Maw said, doing a doughnut in the parking lot and heading us quickly out of town and north toward the city of Beaumont. It was a silent ride, Me-Maw and Aunt Adele watching the road intently, Will breaking the silence with the click of his college class ring against the glass of the window.

In less than thirty minutes Me-Maw pulled to a halt in front of the emergency room doors of St. Elizabeth's Hospital. Will, Aunt Adele, and I rushed out of the car and into the air-conditioning of the emergency room.

Will identified himself to the woman at the desk and was taken down a corridor by a nurse. Aunt Adele and I sat in the emergency waiting room. In a few minutes, the doors opened and Me-Maw rushed in, joining us.

"What you hear?" she asked.

I shook my head. "They took Will back. We don't know anything yet."

So we sat, two old Cajun ladies and I, in a room full of people waiting as we were—for word of a loved one, or to have their own wounds bound.

Finally, a young man in a white jacket came out to us. "Mrs. Broussard?" he asked.

Me-Maw stood up. "That me," she said.

"You Mrs. Romero?" he asked Aunt Adele.

"Yes, sir," she said, standing.

"I'm Dr. Robinson. Mr. DuBois asked that I have the three of you come back."

"Leticia she okay, yeah?" Me-Maw asked.

"Mrs. Broussard, please just come with me."

I took Me-Maw's arm and we followed Dr. Robinson to a small cubicle. Will sat on a gurney, his head in his hands. Dr. Robinson went up to him and touched him lightly on the shoulder. "Mr. DuBois? The ladies are here . . ."

Will looked up. His face told the story. Splotched red from crying, his eyes swollen, his lips thick. I went up and put my arms around him. "I'm sorry," I said.

He held me tight and cried.

Chapter 4

"WELL, YOU ME-MAW GOT A STORY TO TELL FOR SURE, YEAH?"
Paw-Paw said to me as the candy striper wheeled him out of
the hospital and to Me-Maw's waiting Chevy.

"Paw-Paw," I scolded, "this has been hard on everyone.
Me-Maw was very close to Cousin Leticia."

"Pooey," he said, leaning on a crutch as he worked his way
into the front seat of the car, still managing to bang the cast
that covered his leg from his heel to above the knee on the
doorframe of the car. "She ain't seen Leticia since they girls.
And let me tell you somethin', that be a long time, yeah!"
Paw-Paw giggled.

I slammed the door, almost catching his good leg, almost
wishing I had, and walked around the car to the driver's side.
Getting in, I said, "Paw-Paw, you are being a total ass, if you
don't mind my saying so."

"Pooey, girl, you sound jest like you me-maw. Talkin' that
way to a sick man."

"You're not as sick as you're gonna be if anybody but me hears you talking that way about Cousin Leticia."

"Hey, I got nothing against Leticia, 'cept she skinnier than a whittled toothpick. I not the one care she marry that black Cajun. You me-maw the one go crazy 'bout that. Stop talkin' at her. Everthing."

"Me-Maw discovered her, Paw-Paw. It was quite a shock for her."

"You me-maw tougher than she look, girl, I tell you that!"

"So what was the problem anyway, about Cousin Leticia's husband? Why did Me-Maw stop speaking to her?"

Paw-Paw didn't say anything. Finally, I said, "Paw-Paw? I asked you a question."

He sighed. "Girl, they's some things that just be none of you business. And don' go naggin' you me-maw about it none neither."

"What's the big mystery?" I asked.

Paw-Paw shook his head. "Ain't no mystery. Just none of you business, that's all."

I did a little sighing myself and pulled out of the hospital lot.

"You're going to have to direct me, Paw-Paw, I can't remember where you live."

"You ever come see you old paw-paw, maybe you remember, yeah?" he said.

Despite the scolding, Paw-Paw directed me out of St. Mary's Hospital parking lot, right on Ninth Avenue, then left on Gulfway. We stayed on Gulfway through Port Arthur, through the Groves, and then, when Gulfway turns into Highway 87, headed toward the city of Orange. The huge Fina Refinery was on our left, with a canal and marshland between it and the highway. To the right of the highway was more marshland, which eventually led to the Gulf of Mexico. As we got to the old Rainbow Bridge that spanned the

Neches River, about halfway between Port Arthur and Orange, Paw-Paw directed me to turn off the highway, going under the bridge.

It had been almost ten years since I'd been out to the little fishing shack (or camp, as they called them down here) where Paw-Paw had moved after being kicked out of Me-Maw's house. Back then it had just been a bunch of disreputable old cabins hugging the river. Things had changed a bit. A large restaurant now sat at the curve going into the area under the Rainbow Bridge. A marina harboring homemade shrimp boats, cabin cruisers, sailboats, and dilapidated houseboats ringed the cove in front of the restaurant which the road skirted. Inland from the marina was a large area of huge cages, inside which were tall, strange-looking birds.

"An emu farm," Paw-Paw said when I asked.

"You're kidding. Emus?"

"They going for fifteen thousand dollars a pair. Big business. Don't ask me why."

We drove past the marina, emu farm, and restaurant, over a cattle guard and off the paved road onto a crushed-oyster-shell road, leading us down under the bridge where Paw-Paw lived. I noticed a few new houses—nicer ones built on stilts, but the old ones I remembered were still there—the trailer with the built-on front lean-to covered with telephone transformers and obscured by junk; a small trailer with a shed over it for the safety of the boat. I remember Paw-Paw once telling me that the trailer roof had started to leak and, instead of fixing it, the owner had built an extension of the shed over the top of the trailer for shelter. Naturally, the better-built shelter was for the boat.

There were a few businesses in the Rainbow Marina now too, a boat lift, an electronics shop, a boat supply, a bait shop in a trailer.

Paw-Paw's house was right next to a Scenic Cruiser bus,

its tires deflated and gray from age, grass growing up to the undercarriage. Paw-Paw's house was a real-live tar-paper shack. A small wooden porch had been pasted on to the front and leaned precariously to the left. The small yard in front of the house had two peacocks pecking aimlessly at the weeds that grew there.

Paw-Paw rolled his window down and yelled, "Scat!" at the peacocks, who looked up, then went on with their business. "I tole that Bartone Skaggs keep them peacocks out my yard! They shit ever'where! And they meaner than sin. Watch where you walk, girl, and don' rile 'em."

I unloaded Paw-Paw and his one scrawny bag and helped him work his way on crutches up the rickety porch and into the house. There was no lock on the door; it would have been a waste of good money, since the doorframe and the door had but a passing acquaintance with each other. The shack was two rooms: a living room/dining room/kitchen and a bedroom/bathroom. I had been in Paw-Paw's house on many occasions, but never for more than a few moments. Usually, when visiting the family, we would stay with Me-Maw in the Groves and drive out to see Paw-Paw under the bridge, picking him up at his house and taking him to dinner in the suburbs or to a movie or whatever. It suddenly hit me that I was actually going to have to sleep in this shack. Excuse me, camp.

The larger of the two rooms was neat and tidy, with a worn sofa and equally worn easy chair. A coffee table and a small TV on a metal stand rounded out the living-room area. An unfinished wood table and two chairs stood in a corner next to a sink, a small refrigerator, and an apartment-sized stove.

I took Paw-Paw's bag into the other room, the bedroom, and took quick note of just what my job of "Paw-Paw sitting" was going to entail. There really wasn't a bathroom. There was an old wooden commode with a pot that slid in and out underneath it. There was also a large galvanized steel wash-tub sitting under a spigot-and-hose contraption coming in from the window. That, I realized, was the bathtub. I had never wanted to be a nurse—I especially had never wanted to be a nurse in the early-nineteenth century.

The bedroom consisted of—other than the antiquated bathroom facilities—a twin-sized iron bed and a dresser. I helped Paw-Paw down on the bed and said I'd go check out the kitchen for dinner. Instead I went into the living room, threw myself on the sprung couch, and cried.

"You hear the one about lil' Judice da Cajun?" Paw-Paw asked between bites of Kentucky Fried Chicken.

"No, and I don't want to," I said. I was being decidedly ungracious. I didn't want to hear any stupid Cajun jokes. I didn't want to feel guilty about serving KFC instead of a four-course Cajun dinner. I didn't want to sleep on the couch. I didn't want to do my business and then carry it out-side. I didn't want to bathe in a washtub. And I just plain didn't want to be there. It was hot, humid, and the smell of the marsh and the river and the refinery was enough to give me flu symptoms: headache, nausea, and the urge to get the hell out of Dodge.

"Big Maurice come upon lil' Judice holding his hands over his ears real hard and big Maurice he say, 'Hey, lil' Judice, what you doin'?' and lil' Judice he say, 'Tryin' to hold on to a thought,'" Paw-Paw said, and laughed like an idiot.

I glared at him.

"Girl, you got no sense a humor," Paw-Paw said. "Don' see how you be a comedian, no. You tell me a joke you so dam' funny, yeah?"

"I don't feel like telling jokes," I said.

Paw-Paw put his chicken down on his plate and stood up with the help of his crutches. "Girl, I don' need you help. I been takin' care myself thirty-five year, I think I can do that a lil' bit longer. You go on back wherever you suppose to be. I take care myself, I tell you that!"

"Paw-Paw, don't be silly, you have a broken leg—"

"I don' need charity an' I don' need you actin' like me and mine ain't good nuff for you! You go on back wherever you suppose to be!"

"Paw-Paw!"

He went into the bedroom and slammed the door. I fell back in my chair and tried to think of alternatives. I could move him into Me-Maw's house.

But only over her dead body.

I could get him transported somehow to Austin, schlep him up the stairs to my garage apartment . . . forget that noise. My parents' house! I could get him to Austin somehow. I had the key to their house and, after all, it was my mother's turn to be taking care of him anyway! Great idea.

Then I remembered Will. Will was in Port Arthur. Will was hurt, grieving, troubled. Will needed me. Or so I hoped.

Paw-Paw needed me. I felt sorry for both of them. I'm not the kind of person one would wish for in need. I am not particularly sympathetic, empathetic, or handy in a crisis. I never wanted to grow up to be a nurse, a teacher, or even a mother. I'm not the nurturing sort.

I knew those things about myself. I knew I wasn't Florence Nightingale, or even Nurse Ratchett. And I also knew above all else that I needed to go to the bathroom. Paw-Paw was in the room where the john was, and after his grand exit I didn't think he'd be particularly gracious about me barging in and asking him to leave.

I looked out the small window at the back of the shack toward the river. To the right of the shack was a smaller shack—with a quarter-moon cut into the door. I figured it beat the hell out of squatting in the front yard with the peacocks.

I opened the rickety back door and jumped to the ground, as Paw-Paw hadn't seen fit, for some reason, to put in a step, and walked toward the outhouse. Just as I got there the door opened and out stepped a man of about eighty, smaller than I, zipping his fly as he walked. He smiled and bowed his head several times toward me. I smiled and bowed back. He was Asian; Vietnamese, I assumed. Great, I thought, a communal outhouse. But need being what it was, I went in anyway.

  I didn't see Paw-Paw the rest of that evening, and spent part of the time studying his walls—something I hadn't done since I was a little girl. Looking at Paw-Paw's walls brought back my love for him, my bond with him.

One whole wall of Paw-Paw's shack was covered with framed photographs—but not the kind Me-Maw had; not photos of children and grandchildren and great-grandchildren. Paw-Paw's photos were about Port Arthur, his adopted home, and made me remember why I was where I was at that moment.

One was a tall, thin framed shot of the Spindletop Gusher that blew on January 10, 1901. This was the gusher that caused Port Arthur to become one of the greatest oil-refining centers in the world. Back when there was still oil to refine. The picture next to it was of Spindletop one year after the first gusher blew—a picture of mile upon mile of oil derricks. I remember Paw-Paw telling me, when I was little, with awe in his voice, that one hundred thousand barrels of oil a day were produced there.

Then there was a picture of Pleasure Island in its heyday, a strip of land between Port Arthur and the Gulf of Mexico—Port Arthur's answer to Coney Island. I used to love to look at those pictures when I was little, at the people in their funny clothes and silly bathing costumes, and pretend that I could go back to that time.

But the last pictures were the ones that always fascinated me. The pictures of the Texas City blast. An oil-refinery town like Port Arthur, Texas City is located between Houston and Galveston, and the force of the blast that day, back in 1947, when chemicals aboard a ship docked in the canal exploded, could be felt as far as Port Arthur, over one hundred miles away. The kinship with that town so far away wasn't just that some of the same companies that populated Port Arthur had refineries there; and it wasn't just because a few people from Port Arthur were there that day and lost their lives; and it wasn't because the blast, seventy-five miles away, was so strong it shook buildings in Port Arthur and the residents, Me-Maw and Paw-Paw included, could stand outside and see the blaze when they looked to the southwest.

No, the connection was the brotherhood. It was a refinery town, just like Port Arthur. A place that relied on oil and oilmen to make the livings of those who resided there. And a place that knew, like Port Arthur did, and still does, that one day this could happen. One day hell could rain down upon the town and take away everything. Everyone in Port Arthur, just like everyone in Texas City and every other refinery town in this country and elsewhere, knew he lived twenty-four hours a day, seven days a week, with a living, breathing monster that was stilled only if everyone always did his job—and did it correctly.

There's something horribly fascinating about that kind of destruction, and I remember as a child staring at those pictures for hours: at a torn-apart house with a huge hole in the front yard where a piece of the propeller shaft from a ship had buried itself in the ground almost a mile from the explosion site; at homes with blazing fires and black smoke billowing in the background. The accounts of the dead and dying rose to twelve hundred in some reports.

Paw-Paw had worked in the Texas Company refinery for almost fifty years, and oil and what it wrought were close to his heart, as his picture gallery showed.

I finally turned my back on Paw-Paw's gallery and lay down on the couch, spending a fitful night trying to sleep on the old relic.

The next morning I woke up with my monthly friend. I cleaned up at the kitchen sink, sank down into the couch and pouted. How was I supposed to deal with the needs of my monthly with no proper bathroom facilities? How come, in 1992, I was stuck in a bad imitation of *God's Little Acre*?

I heard Paw-Paw stirring in the other room, but didn't feel quite up to doing anything about it. I sat huddled on the sofa feeling sorry for myself.

When Paw-Paw hobbled in on his crutches, heading for the kitchen area and his coffeepot, I said, "Paw-Paw, we have to do something. I can't live like this—with an outhouse! Maybe we should move you to a motel."

"Outhouse?" Paw-Paw said. He looked out the window toward the quarter-moon receptacle. "You been using Ho's outhouse?"

"What?"

"Why you do that, girl?"

"You were in the bedroom . . ."

"So? Why you not use this?" he asked, walking to a door in the kitchen area and opening it. I followed and looked in—at the loveliest bathroom I'd ever seen. It had a bathtub, a sink, and the most beautiful white porcelain flush commode in the world.

"Paw-Paw, it's a bathroom!"

He said, "Pooey!" shook his head, and moved into the living-room area, sitting down on the old armchair. "You think I don't got a bathroom? You ever come visit me for more than three minute at a time, you see I got a bathroom. I built it my own self back five year ago. I got a kitchen too. I even drive a car when my leg ain't broke! What you think, I some kinda rube?"

"Excuse me," I said, heading in and closing the door.

When I came out I made coffee silently and silently poured him a cup of the strongest coffee I'd ever made.

Paw-Paw took a sip and spit it back into the cup. "You always make dishwater, girl?" He handed me the coffee pot, got up and walked into the kitchen indicating that I should follow. Once there he had me pour the entire pot down the sink. "I see now we gonna have some troubles, yeah? You don' even know how to make coffee, girl, what you mama teach you, eh?" He looked at me standing in the living room. "Well," he said, motioning toward me with his head. "Get over here. I teach you to make coffee Cajun-style, yeah?"

A little after noon the phone rang. Paw-Paw was resting in the bedroom and I picked up the old black dial-type phone. A real antique. "Hello?"

"Kimmey?" a voice asked.

"Yes."

"It's Will."

I sat down on the straight chair next to the phone table. "Hi," I said, "how are you?"

He sighed. "Not great. The funeral is tomorrow. Will you come?"

"Yes, of course. Anything I can do for you before that . . ."

"Well, there is something."

"Anything," I said.

"It seems like such a trivial thing and I wouldn't do it now except . . . Well, I live in an apartment complex and we're only allowed one parking spot each. And I've got my mother's car here . . . I've got to move it. Management's put notices all over it saying they're going to tow it away. Anyway, there's this guy in Nederland with a car lot who'll give me a fair price. I just need you to follow me over there while I drive Mom's . . ."

"Sure," I said. "No problem." He gave me directions and we set a time, an hour from then, and I went to tell Paw-Paw where I was going.

"Well, you din' say nothin' 'bout needing the car today, girl, so I tole Ho he could use it to go to Houston 'bout his status. They got his papers all mess up there. He gotta go fix it. I say take my car, we don' need it, yeah? So the car ain't here, girl."

I looked out the window. Yep. The car ain't here. I called Will and explained the situation.

He sighed. "Okay, look. I'll come out there and get you, then we'll come back here and get Mom's car, and you can follow in my car, okay?"

"Will, I'm sorry . . ."

"It can't be helped. I'll be there in half an hour." With that he hung up.

⤷ "What do you mean, you can't drive my car?" Will said. His hands were on his hips and his face was flushed. He was under a lot of strain and I seemed to be adding to it.

We were standing under the covered parking lot at the back of his apartment complex, a large rambling wood-shingle affair, the kind of complex architecture that had been outlawed in most major cities because of the potential fire hazard.

We both looked at his car—a snazzy little Japanese number, low to the ground, silver in color with black interior, a CD player, lots of knobs and levers, and a five-speed gear shift.

"I can't drive standard," I said, bowing my head in shame.

"You what?"

"I can't drive standard," I said again, louder.

"I heard you," he said. He laughed slightly. "You can't drive standard?"

"No." I bowed my head again.

"Unbelievable." Will shook his head and then handed me the keys to his mother's larger-than-necessary Buick. "How about an automatic?"

I smiled. "That I can handle."

"Good. You take Mom's car and I'll lead in mine."

I agreed and got behind the wheel of the Buick, following Will out of the complex and left on the Beaumont Highway toward the small town of Nederland. When we got to the light on the corner of Thirty-ninth and I-10, I hit the brake too hard, causing the Buick to jerk to a stop. A jar rolled out from under the passenger side of the front seat, rolling back and fourth on the floor mat. I leaned down to pick it up. It took the full length of the traffic light for the contents of the jar to register in my brain. When they did I just sat there, not moving the car after the light had turned green. The car behind me honked loud and long, bringing me out of my daze. I moved the car forward, speeding to catch up with Will. Coming up alongside him, I motioned for him to follow me and led him to the parking lot of a Popeye's Fried Chicken.

Will got out of his car, slamming the door louder than

necessary, and poked his head in the lowered window of the passenger side door. "Now what?" he said.

I held up the jar. Inside were two dead wasps.

༄ "So the stupid cop—excuse me, stupid policeman, says, 'So? It's like a couple of dead wasps,' and I said, 'Yes, and she died of anaphylactic shock', and he says—"

Pucci interrupted with, "So you're insinuating the old broad got offed?"

"Delicately put, Pucci, but yes, that's what I'm saying. Not insinuating, mind you; I'm saying it outright."

"Couldn't the wasps have gotten stuck in the jar when they got in her car to sting her in the first place?"

"Two? Maybe one wasp, but two?"

"Seems like an iffy way to murder someone and how come those two were still in the jar, huh? Why didn't they fly out with their buddies and help do in the old broad?"

I stretched out on the bed, as far as the phone cord would let me. I was at Me-Maw's house, Cousin Norvella Paw-Paw-sitting. I had the hall phone stretched into the spare room for privacy in talking with Pucci. "Me-Maw—"

"Beg pardon?"

I sighed. "My grandmother—"

"Me-Maw?"

"It's a Cajun thing. Anyway—"

"Me-Maw?" Pucci laughed.

"Can it, Pucci. My *grandmother* says Cousin Leticia was always allergic to insect stings, and everybody knew it. So—"

"So somebody comes up to her in the car and says, 'Hey, Leticia, honey, you wanna sit right here for a few minutes while I empty this jar of deadly wasps on you? Thanks a lot.' And that still doesn't explain why those two were still in the jar. Maybe Leticia always carried dead wasps in her car!"

I lay quietly for a moment, in the pissed-off silence that came with any extended conversation with Detective Sal Pucci. "Maybe those wasps died before the others were let out! If they were already dead, then they wouldn't be able to fly out, now would they?"

"It's still an iffy way to off somebody," Pucci said in his most belligerent tone.

"She was tired. She was asleep in the car. She was—" I sat bolt upright on the bed. "She was drugged!"

Pucci laughed again. "Now this is getting good. What? A jealous lover?"

"Maybe. There was this old harpy at the reunion. Someone who had run off with Leticia's husband years before . . ."

"Years before. How many years before?"

I stretched back out on the bed. "I don't know. Thirty, something like that."

"So she runs off with this woman's husband thirty years ago and decides now's a good time to off the old broad. Is that what you're saying?"

I twisted the spiral telephone cord round and round my finger. "I don't know who or why—yet. But I will. I solved that case in Chicago, right?"

"Lady, you almost died in Chicago."

"So I've learned something since then. All I'm asking you is this: Could this be murder?"

There was a long silence. Finally, Pucci said, "Yeah, babe, it could be murder."

"Okay, so call these stupid cops down here and tell them that!"

He snorted laughter. "Yeah, right. Some damn Yankee cop calls them and says, 'Get on the ball,' what do you think's going to happen?"

I sat up again, determination straightening my shoulders and putting a light in my eye. (I'm sure.) "Then I'll just have to solve it myself."

"Kruse, stay out of it, okay?"

"Are you serious? Do you really expect me to listen to this?"

Pucci sighed. "Not any more than you did last time. Okay, look. I've got some vacation time coming, I'll come down there . . ."

My mind raced over the possibilities of Pucci and Will in the same town, with me thrown in there someplace. The idea nauseated me. "No. Absolutely not. Port Arthur, Texas, is not the vacation capital of the world. You'd have a terrible time. Besides, I can handle this—"

"Kruse!"

"I won't do anything you wouldn't approve of. I'll call you at every juncture."

"You'd better."

"I will."

Pucci sighed again. "I've grown accustomed to your wicked ways, kid. I don't want anything to happen to you."

I was touched, almost to the point of tears. Then he added, "If you die, what excuse would I have for calling Phoebe?"

Chapter

5

THE ONLY THING BLACK I HAD WITH ME (AND, IN FACT, THE ONLY thing black I own) are a pair of Bill Blass long johns. They're incredibly cute and I look great in them, but they're not exactly appropriate for a funeral. So I borrowed. From Paw-Paw, I got a pair of black dress pants fashionably baggy and shiny-seated; from Paw-Paw's neighbor Ho, I got a black silk tunic with mandarin collar; and in Me-Maw's attic I found an incredibly cool, 1930s-style cloche hat which, when worn at the proper angle, not only covered what there was of my hair but gave me a very Joan-Crawfordish look. I belted the black silk tunic with a multicolored scarf, bloused the top, and looked in the mirror.

Except for the pink high-tops, I looked great. Borrowing Paw-Paw's car, I drove to the nearest Payless and spent my third-to-the-last twenty-dollar bill on a pair of two-inch black pumps and some dark hose. Then I drove to Me-Maw's to pick her up for the funeral.

By the time we got to Me-Maw's church in the Groves, I had a carload: Me-Maw, Aunt Adele, Cousin Norvella, and Norvella's oldest, Jesse, who was deemed old enough for funerals.

When we walked into the strangely quiet but semi-full church, Will was the only one sitting in the front. We all trooped up there to sit with him. He had decided to have his mother buried in Port Arthur rather than in her home of Armentine, Louisiana, so he could be near her grave. Me-Maw was only too happy to make all the arrangements at her church. Leticia may have fled the Catholic faith late in life, but Me-Maw was determined to bring her back into the fold—dead or alive. Okay, actually dead.

A few relatives had come in from Armentine, but they were even more distantly related than we were. No one seemed to mind that we took up the two front rows.

I held Will's hand through the entire service—which seemed to take hours and hours and probably actually did. It was what Catholics call a high mass, which means it takes a lot longer than a regular mass and everybody feels he got his money's worth.

At Will's request, Norvella drove Paw-Paw's car to the cemetery while Me-Maw, Aunt Adele, and I rode with Will in the funeral home's limo. There was an awning over the hole into which Cousin Leticia's body would be laid to rest, but that didn't keep the nearly one-hundred-degree heat from almost frying me in my black silk and serge. Sweat ran down my face from under the wool cloche hat and the little burgundy paper flower on the band wilted. My armpits were dripping, my shoes were too tight, and my butt itched from Paw-Paw's suit pants. But still the priest went on and on.

Finally we were released, shovels full of earth were laid over Cousin Leticia, and we headed for the cars.

"I need to drive everyone back," I told Will at the door of the limo.

"I know," he said. He took my hand. "I don't know if I would have gotten through this without you, Kimmey."

I smiled. "You would have. But I'm glad I was here for you anyway."

He leaned down, way down, and kissed me on the side of the mouth. "I'll call you in a few days," he said.

I nodded, squeezed his hand, and walked back to where the ladies awaited me.

I turned back for just one more look and saw Will with a woman in a floor-length, full-skirted, ruffled black dress, black gloves, and a large black hat covered with netting. The permed blond hair and abundance of makeup gave me the hint Will was being love-bombed by Cousin Barbara Sue. Except neither was smiling. I could hear their voices but not their words—and the voices told me the words were not kind ones of condolence and acceptance. Will and Cousin Barbara Sue were fighting. And I wished I knew what about.

"Well, if we're all gonna die from the heat, at least we're in the right place!" Cousin Norvella's loud voice boomed from the back seat of Paw-Paw's car. "You gonna drive or stand around admiring the scenery?"

Once in the car, Me-Maw started in. "Oo-eee, you see that, Adele, I don't believe it, no!"

Aunt Adele went "tsk, tsk". "She got some nerve, yeah? Comin' to Leticia's funeral!"

"Who? Barbara Sue?" I asked.

"What Barbara Sue? She family! I'm talking about that Dorisca Judice, that who!" Me-Maw said, her voice raised. "Runnin' that woman through the middle with a cane knife be too good for her, I tell you what!"

"Dorisca was at the services?" I asked. I hadn't been looking around, paying too much attention to Will's needs to notice who else was in the house.

"I don't know 'bout that," Me-Maw said, "but at the cemetery, she be standing out like a fart in church, I tell you what!"

"Wearin' red to a funeral, Lord Almighty," Aunt Adele said.

"You talking about that tacky woman in the blond beehive and the red dress?" Cousin Norvella asked, resplendent in too-tight black stretch pants and a black-and-white sweater shell with armholes so big you could see her white bra with her arms down.

"That the one," Me-Maw said. "She just be coming ta make sure Leticia be dead, yeah?"

Ho was baby-sitting Paw-Paw, so I took time to eat at Me-Maw's. It's a rare day that I would willingly give up a meal at Me-Maw's. To my credit, I did stuff a few gar-balls (don't ask—they're delicious but you really don't want to know what they're made of) and some fried okra in Paw-Paw's suit pants pockets to take home to him. After all, the man had been living for two days off my cooking. He deserved something edible.

The whole family had shown up at Me-Maw's for the after-funeral goodies—with the exception of Will. Me-Maw had, of course, invited him, but he said he needed to be alone. I was well into my second helping of triple-layer chocolate cake when I heard Suzanne Pleshette behind me.

"Kimberly Anne?"

I turned around and plastered a smile on my face. "Hey, Barbara Sue."

She kissed the air around my face. "Lovely funeral," she

said. "I'd forgotten how beautiful high mass could be. Paganistic, but lovely."

"Jimmy Lynn's not with you?"

She sighed. "Jimmy Lynn and the priest at Me-Maw's church don't get along too well. Why, Father Michael has said just terrible things about our church! Going so far as to remove some of our young people from the congregation!"

I frowned. That sounded weird. "How could he do that?"

Barbara Sue sighed and waved her hand in a gesture of dismissal. "Oh, their parents all went to *his* church, and just because their youngsters decided to seek Jesus in another light, well . . ."

I smiled to myself. Jimmy Lynn got caught proselytizing to the Catholic youth and Father Michael didn't let him get away with it. Go, Father Michael, I thought to myself. But to Barbara Sue I just went "tsk, tsk," then mentally kicked myself for having done it. Oh, please, God, don't let that become a habit!

"It was just terrible," Barbara Sue said. "I feel so sorry for children trying to find the Lord and their parents refusing them admittance to the Kingdom of Heaven."

"Well . . ." I said.

"I'm just so glad you're here in Me-Maw's time of need. She needs all her family with her right now. It's just such a shame your mama and daddy are never around."

I bristled. "They're out of the country right now."

She smiled. "They're so worldly, aren't they?"

I had two choices at that moment, to my way of thinking. I could sock her in the kisser or ask her about her earlier conversation at the cemetery with Cousin Will.

"So," I said, smiling, "you know Cousin Will?"

The wattage of Barbara Sue's smile diminished considerably.

"What?"

"I saw the two of you talking at the cemetery."

"Oh." The wattage moved back up to over one hundred. "Just giving him my condolences. I knew him slightly. We both went to Lamar around the same time."

"Oh, really?"

"Well," Barbara Sue said, moving out of my space, "I need to go home and start dinner for my family. Why, if I wasn't there to feed them, they'd just eat peanut butter or something!" She laughed. "I'm so happy to be a woman, Kimberly Anne. To take care of my family and love them." She patted me on the arm. "One of these days, I just know you'll find that joy for yourself."

She turned and headed out the door before I had a chance to kick her in the shins.

❧ I left Me-Maw's about five, heading back to the bridge and Paw-Paw.

I pulled into the driveway of the shack and shut off the engine, leaning my head back and closing my eyes for just a moment—steeling myself to go inside and hear what Paw-Paw had to say about Me-Maw, my aunts, cousins, and assorted kith and kin. I only stayed that way a moment, though. The mosquitoes found me and decided I was mighty tasty for a city girl. I jumped out of the car and rushed inside, slamming the screen door behind me to keep out the pests.

Too bad someone hadn't done that earlier. Ho and Paw-Paw were sitting at the kitchen table playing a strange Cajun/Vietnamese version of crazy eights. With them, seeming to be having a grand old time, was Detective Sal Pucci of the Chicago PD. Next to Paw-Paw and Ho, Pucci actually looked tall. He also looked strange. He had on a Hawaiian-style shirt—royal-blue background with giant fuchsia-and-yellow flowers all over it—and blue jeans. And, saints preserve us, cowboy boots.

For the almost two weeks I'd known Pucci while in Chicago, I'd never seen him out of a suit. A baggy (though not fashionably so) suit, but a suit. He either had several identical suits or dry-cleaned the one only on his yearly vacation. And it was always worn with a white shirt with a frayed collar, a skinny dark-colored tie, the top botton of the shirt undone and the tie loosened. He wore his hair slicked straight back from his forehead, which further exposed his sexy receding hairline. Funny, before I met Pucci, I'd never considered a receding hairline sexy. As I mentioned, he was not particularly tall—only about five feet five or six—and stockily built. Not my kinda guy at all. I like them tall and thin and tall and well-built and tall and heavy. Basically, I like them tall.

"Hey, *cher*," Paw-Paw said on seeing me (which in true Cajun comes out sounding more like "sha" than the singer's name). "You be back?"

"No, Paw-Paw," I said, "I'm still at the funeral."

"She get like that," Paw-Paw said to Pucci.

"God, do I know that," Pucci said. "Did I tell you what she said when I was trying to save her life back in Chicago?"

Paw-Paw laughed. "Oh, yeah, dat was a good one!"

Ho nodded to me. *He* realized I existed.

I took off my shoes and threw them, my purse, and the cloche hat at the dilapidated sofa. "What are you doing here, Pucci?"

"Take two," Pucci said to Paw-Paw.

Paw-Paw said, "You play a mean crazy eight, Bo." ("Bo" being the Cajun equivalent of "Mac" or "Bud" or "Hey, you.")

He put down a two and turned to Ho, saying something in

Cajun. Ho took four cards off the deck and replied in what sounded like Vietnamese. Paw-Paw laughed.

"Pucci?" I said.

Never taking his eyes off the game, Pucci said, "Hum?"

I was hot. I'd been bitten numerous times by bloodthirsty mosquitoes the size of Buicks, my feet hurt, I smelled, and I'd basically had enough. I marched over to Pucci and took the top of one ear firmly between thumb and forefinger and lifted. Not being a complete idiot, Pucci came up with the ear. I marched him thusly out the door into the front yard.

Knowing I now had his complete attention, I let go of his ear and said, "What are you doing here?"

"Great hairdo," Pucci said. He grinned. In better days that grin had been known to make me a little queasy with lust—lust kept well under control, I might add. It was not having that effect upon me at the moment. I made a move toward him, mayhem in my heart, and stepped in my stockinged foot into a pile of peacock shit.

"Oh, gross!" I wailed, dancing on one foot back to the front steps, where I desperately tried to wipe it off on the bottom rung. Which I, of course, would now always think of as the dung rung. I looked up to see Pucci laughing his ass off. Very quietly I said, "I hate you."

"No, you don't," Pucci said, grinning.

I stood up and turned. "Oh, but I do. I really, really do." I hip-hopped into the house, slamming the screen door behind me, trying to keep my dirty foot off the floor, and headed into the bathroom. I heard the screen door slam again.

"No, you don't," Pucci called as I firmly closed the door to the bathroom. "You really, really don't."

*   *   *

Paw-Paw's house at night was almost like camping out. All the windows were open for air and you didn't want to put on too many lights because that would attract bugs through the large holes in the screens. In the past two days, I'd come to know a certain kind of peace in Paw-Paw's living room at night. I'd get him in bed and have the living room to myself—and sit there listening to the frogs and crickets and katydids making their nightly music. The breeze from the river would rattle the leaves in the pecan trees and sometimes I could hear the far-off laughter of night fishermen, all these sounds breaking through the steady drone of the refinery less than a mile away.

That night did not fall into the pattern. That night Pucci was there.

"What are you doing here?"

"I've never been in Texas before," he said. "To a Chicagoan, Texas is an exotic place to vacation."

"Bull."

Paw-Paw was in bed and Ho had gone home for the night. It was just Pucci and me and the mosquitoes.

"You are very ungracious, Kruse, you know that?"

"Ungracious?" I snorted with derision. Really. "You came down here to check up on me!"

He touched a hand to his breast in a gesture of innocence, thought better of it and said, "So? What's wrong with that?"

"Did you ever think that an invitation might be in order here? Did you ever stop to think that possibly you might not be wanted?"

"Now I'm hurt. Really. To the quick." Pucci leaned back lazily in his chair and grinned at me.

"Where do you plan on spending the night?" I demanded. "Because if you think—"

"It's all worked out. Don't worry your pretty little head about it." He stood and stretched. "Speaking of which—you want the floor or the couch?" He grinned. "Or maybe we could both fit on the couch. You're small."

I stood up. "Pucci—"

He headed for the back door. "Ho graciously invited me to spend a few days with him in the Scenic Cruiser. That should be a trip."

"How do you know that? As far as I can tell, Ho doesn't speak English."

"Your paw-paw told me so."

"Oh." I still hadn't figured out yet how the two communicated—but somehow they managed. Then the reality of what Pucci had said struck home. "A few days?"

"Or weeks. Or whatever." And he was gone, jumping out the back door as if he were used to it. God, how I hated Pucci.

⤙ My relationship with Pucci was, is, and always will be adversarial, tempered with unrequited lust. We spent most of the two weeks in Chicago sniping at each other—when we weren't looking longingly into each other's eyes. He only kissed me once. At the end. Right before I left. It wasn't even a very passionate kiss. It was a sweet kiss. A tender kiss. An "I'm-glad-it's-all-over-and-you're-still-alive" kiss. Which, unfortunately, still made my toes curl and my ovaries stand at attention.

But he wasn't my type. Cousin Will was my type: tall, gorgeous, and wounded. As I said, I'm not good at binding wounds, but I seemed to be strangely attracted to men with open, running, oozing emotional boo-boos. Show me a man who has just been dumped by the love of his life, had his car repossessed, his business fail, and his dog run over, and I'll fall madly in love.

But there was more to Will than just that. He hadn't been

wounded when I'd fallen madly in lust. With Will it was chemistry. The real McCoy. The stuff through which better living is made. Chemistry with a capital *C*.

And he was sweet. Pucci was anything but sweet. Will was sensitive—Pucci was an emotional bull in a china shop. Will was kind and thoughtful and intelligent—Pucci was abrasive, thoughtless, and street-smart. The only thing Pucci had going over Will was the big one: He wasn't related to me.

These were the thoughts that kept me tossing and turning on Paw-Paw's couch. These were the thoughts that made me call Phoebe at two-thirty in the morning.

∕℘ "Do you do this because you get a better rate in the middle of the night," Phoebe said, "or do you do it because you think large bags under my eyes are a fashion statement?"

"Pucci's here," I said. That shut her up. There was a moment of stunned silence as she contemplated my words.

"Here where?" she finally said.

"Here in the house, except he's not, he's next door with Ho."

"I'm sure that makes sense to someone," Phoebe said, audibly yawning.

So I told her about the funeral, about Will, about my murder theory, about Cousin Norvella's bra, and about Pucci, not leaving out how he was dressed. She'd never, of course, met or even seen Pucci, but details have never been something Phoebe and I have endeavored to keep out of our conversations.

"Why does he claim to be there?" Phoebe the attorney said.

"He claims he's on vacation. Tomorrow he'll probably claim he's here because of the murder."

"Which is, of course, not the real reason?"

"Of course not," I said. "The real reason Pucci's here is because of Cousin Will."

"Aha," Phoebe said. She is the possessor of the most sarcastic "aha" you've ever heard. "Jealousy being the chief ingredient here, I assume?"

I didn't like her tone. Of course jealousy was the chief ingredient, anyone could see that. Pucci had come all the way from Chicago to Port Arthur, Texas, simply because I'd mentioned another man's name over the phone. During a conversation in which he had accused *me* of being jealous of him and Phoebe. And now, by Pheobe's tone of voice, it was obvious that *she* was jealous of my relationship with Pucci. The truth of the matter was that there were many layers of jealousy going on here—the only one that wasn't accurate was my being jealous of Pucci and Phoebe. As if I'd care if there *was* something going on between the two, which there definitely wasn't because they hadn't even met. And, if I had anything to say about it, they never would.

And now here Phoebe was using this proprietary tone of voice about Pucci. This had happened before, of course. One cannot be friends with someone from junior high through eternity without a few squabbles over men. Phoebe was completely in the wrong here. She'd never even met the man. I'd spent the night with him. He was mine. I didn't want him, but he was mine. She couldn't have him.

"You know, you're right," I finally said. "I think I will stop calling you in the middle of the night. You can be very peckish in the wee hours, did you know that?"

"Peckish? Peckish? You wanna see peckish?" And she hung up.

I replaced the receiver gently and went back to lie down on the couch, feeling lonely but righteous.

Chapter

6

"So big Maurice he come upon lil' Judice standing there at the filling station jest shaking his head in wonderment," Paw-Paw said. "And big Maurice he say, 'Lil' Judice, what you be doing?' And lil' Judice he say, 'Ain't it jest grand the way these fellas know jest where to put their pumps so's they can get gas!'"

Paw-Paw laughed, Pucci laughed, and I dumped two bowls of oatmeal on the table. Luckily, before Pucci could counterattack Paw-Paw's joke, the phone rang. I went to answer it.

"Hello?" I said.

"You're a bitch," Phoebe said.

"So are you," I said.

"The only reason I'm calling you is that Bob Randerson at the bank called this morning looking for you."

"Oh, joy." Bob Randerson was my personal banker and gave me a lot more personal attention than someone with a high three-figure checking account usually gets. His personal attention ran to repeated offers of good rates on money-market accounts, drinks, and bed. I've consistently declined all three. "What did he want?"

"According to Randerson, you've got a balance of three dollars and forty-seven cents and outstanding checks coming in as of this morning totaling four hundred eighty-five dollars and seventy-three cents."

"Oh, shit."

"He's holding them, and I've authorized him to move a thousand from my account into yours."

Great. Now I *owed* her something. I hate being indebted to Phoebe because she's always so *nice* about it. After our fight the night before, I didn't feel like being beholden to her for anything. On the other hand, I had forty dollars in cash in my purse, nothing in savings, and no job in the foreseeable future.

"Thank you," I finally said. Grudgingly.

"It was nothing." Which, indeed, I knew it to be. Phoebe was an attorney with a very lucrative corporate practice. She could spend half that much having a bikini wax and lunch.

"No, really," I said, "I appreciate it."

"You need to get a job, though, Kimberly."

Advice and "Kimberly." She was truly pissed. As if I cared.

"Doing what, Phoebe Rainbow?" I asked. I can get just as pissy as she, any day of the week. (Although she was named at birth Phoebe Saperstein Lowe, her parents legally had her name changed after their attendance at Woodstock, when Phoebe was two years old, to Phoebe Rainbow Love. Although she later legally dropped the a-i-n-b-o-w and just goes by the initial, I like to mention it from time to time to keep her humble.)

"A job is a job, Kimberly."

"You're suggesting McDonald's perhaps?"

"You're too good to work at McDonald's?"

"I'm too good to be having this conversation. Thank you for the money. Good-bye." And I hung up. Loudly.

"You ladies having a tiff?" Pucci asked.

"Butt out, Pucci."

He stood up from the table. "Maybe I should call Phoeb and make sure she's okay."

"Fine," I said. At which point I truly lost my cool. I ripped the cord to the antique phone out of the wall and threw the damned thing at Pucci. Then I slammed out the back door, jumped to the ground, and walked rapidly toward the river.

Water tends to soothe me. Even this water—tepid, smelly, with things floating in it I'd just as soon not identify. But it was water. And water usually did the trick. I was not having a good month. I'd lost the TV gig, I was baby-sitting my grandfather, Pucci was in my own backyard (literally), we won't mention my hair, I was dead broke, had no job prospects, and now my best friend in the entire world hated me. And all over a man. A man I didn't even want.

So, I thought, take a weekend off. Drive to Austin. With Pucci. Introduce him to Phoebe. Let them fall in love. It was the sisterly thing to do. It was the right thing to do. Maybe I'd get Will to come up for the weekend, too, and we could make it a foursome.

Thinking of Will made me think of his mother. Poor Cousin Leticia. Was I the only one who thought it was murder? The Port Arthur police didn't think so. I don't even think Will really thought so. He was just placating me. Pucci was the only one who could see the truth as I saw it. One dead wasp in a jar could be an accident. Two definitely spelled murder. And the only way someone could murder Cousin Leticia by putting wasps in her car was if she was in a deep sleep, so nothing much would wake her. And the only way she could have been in such a deep sleep was if she had been drugged.

I thought back to the events just before Leticia went to her car. We hadn't eaten yet, so there was no way she could have ingested drugs with her food—besides, it was a communal pot, with everybody eating from the same dishes. A dicey way to drug someone. Then I remembered—all of us standing there with drinks. I with my diet Coke and Cousin Leticia with her Big Red.

The Big Red had to be how she got it. Someone had spiked her soda. Who had been around? Everybody. But one person stood out in my mind like—as Me-Maw would say—a fart in church. Dorisca Judice. She was there right before Leticia started getting sleepy, and she was the only one at the reunion—to my knowledge—who would have anything against Leticia. Arguably, it would have made more sense if Cousin Leticia had murdered Dorisca, since Dorisca's the one who ran off with Leticia's man—not the other way around—but . . .

And then, of course, there was Barbara Sue, the hair-spray queen. I knew she'd lied about her conversation with Will at the cemetery the day before. The looks on both their faces and the sound of both their voices were not the looks and sounds of condolences being given and received. And Leticia had reacted strangely to Barbara Sue. I'd put it off to Barbara Sue's epidemic proselytizing, but Cousin Leticia, according to Me-Maw, was born again, too. That wouldn't put her off. That would bring them closer together. But there had been something . . .

I felt a nudge in my back. I didn't have to turn around to know it was Pucci. I could smell him. That Old Spice/Aqua Velva smell mixed with garlic. Did Phoebe have any idea what she was letting herself in for?

"What?" I said.

"That's my question. As in, what's eating you, short-stuff?"

"Nothing. I was just thinking about Cousin Leticia."

"The old broad who got offed?" Pucci said.

I sighed. "Yes, Pucci, as you so delicately put it."

"Or should I say your wanna-be late mother-in-law?"

I turned around and glared at him. It was ten o'clock in the morning and sweat was pouring off both of us. The pecan trees stood still as death in the breezeless morning air and the sun beat down through the refinery haze with a temperature in the mid-nineties.

I reached up and flicked off a drop of sweat before it went into Pucci's eyes. "I told you Port Arthur wasn't a vacation paradise."

His face serious as major surgery, Pucci said, "Anywhere you are is paradise, Kruse." Then, of course, he laughed.

I passed him and headed for the back door of the shack.

"Where you going, Kruse?" he called after me.

"Anywhere you're not."

I grabbed the handle of the back door and pulled myself up over the threshold, went inside and sat down with the morning paper.

☙ There it was, bigger than life on the same page with the Want Ads. An advertisement for "What a Hoot Defensive Driving." "Got a ticket? Need a break on your insurance? But tired of the dull, boring defensive-driving classes? Try What a Hoot and get a hoot out of defensive driving with our instructors who are actual stand-up comics! Why not enjoy your punishment! Call What a Hoot today!"

I'm a certified defensive-driving instructor, certified by the State of Texas. Two years ago, not long after starting to work the comedy clubs, I did a six-month stint at a comedy defensive-driving school in Austin. They paid for the accreditation and I did all the requisite classroom training and student teaching, and since then have kept up my accreditation.

It was a good gig for a beginning comedian. Before I started it, my idea of dealing with a heckler in the audience was a judicious "Oh, yeah?" Working with a truly captive—and sober—audience of up to fifty people who are spending what they consider a wasted Saturday, you have to learn to deal with heckles and comebacks because it's all part of the show. The joy of audience participation. And you have to stay on your feet or they could turn on you in a New York minute.

And as I remembered it, the money was good—five bucks a head—and if you have a full class (the Texas Education Association [TEA] rules allow a maximum of fifty people per session), you could make up to $250 a class. Considering that amount is a week's salary with some clubs, it's not a bad gig at all. Four classes and I could pay back Phoebe. Eight classes and I'd have a bankroll. Sixteen classes and I could run off to Tahiti.

I got down on my hands and knees and plugged the phone line back into the wall jack, stood up, picked up the phone, and dialed.

They loved me. They wanted me. They desired me. And who, of course, could blame them? I was the first actual professional comedian to apply for a job with What a Hoot. They were ecstatic. And willing to pay me the highest salary of any of their comedian/instructors—a whopping $3.50 per student in classes that usually ran no more than twenty to twenty-five people. Okay, so it would take a little longer to pay back Phoebe. A little longer for a bankroll. And most of my life to run off to Tahiti. It still beat being a "Can I help you?" girl at McDonald's.

I found Paw-Paw's car in the parking lot, one of several multi-colored, multi-bruised ancient Chevys, started it and headed out of the lot. I stopped at the entrance to the Beaumont Highway to let a string of cars go by. Fourth in line was a 1965 Mustang convertible, cherry red and cherry condition. The woman driving it was entirely too old for it, with a beehive of bleached-blond hair covered with a garish scarf, big Audrey-Hepburn-in-*Charade* sunglasses, and a hot-pink top that clashed terribly with the cherry-red Mustang.

It took a full minute for my mind to register that the woman who'd just passed me on the Beaumont Highway was Dorisca Judice. I pulled into the line of traffic, gingerly passing cars to get behind the Mustang. The vanity plates read FOXXXX. In another lifetime maybe, I thought. I'd assumed Dorisca lived in Armentine, where Cousin Leticia and the nasty Armand had lived when he ran off with Dorisca. But that had been thirty years ago. Maybe she lived in Port Arthur now. More reason for old Enic to think he could get away with bringing her to the family reunion.

The Mustang turned west on Thirty-fourth Street and I followed, slowing down and letting a car get between Dorisca's and mine. I'd seen that once on a "Magnum, P.I." rerun. There's very little to do during the day in hotel rooms while you're waiting for your nightly gig. I could recite dialogue verbatim from "The Brady Bunch," if anybody ever asked. So far, no one has. With a few drinks in me, I've been known to sing the theme song to "The Patty Duke Show" in its entirety.

The Mustang turned into a street off Thirty-fourth. The car between us didn't and I had to take the chance Dorisca wasn't paying much attention. From what I'd seen, she seemed to use her rearview mirror exclusively for checking her lipstick, not for checking traffic.

Half a block down, she turned into a driveway. I drove on to the end of the block and pulled over to the side, turning around in my seat. Dorisca was just getting out of the car. The hot-pink gauzy top fell to mid-butt over matching hot-pink stretch pants, the stirrups of which could be seen going into her hot-pink three-inch pumps. She took the scarf off her head, throwing it into the car, patted her hair, picked up a gigantic purse off the passenger seat, and turned for the front door of the house. Using a key, she opened the door and entered. Either her own home or the home of someone she knew very well.

I turned the oversized Chevy around in an empty driveway and slowly drove by the house, noting the street number. I'd have to go back to the corner of Thirty-fourth and get the name of the street, which I hadn't noticed when turning onto it.

The house was a typical two-bedroom frame bungalow, painted white with faded blue shutters. Along the ditch there were tires painted white and buried halfway into the ground, with petunias growing in the middle. The front yard was splendorous with roadside gewgaws: a miniature wooden windmill, about four feet high; ceramic glazed frogs, five of them, in a circle around two pink flamingos; a lawn jockey by the front door; a shrine with the Virgin Mary in one corner of the yard, surrounded by a rock and cactus garden; and four wind socks in varying degrees of cute hanging from the rafters of the front porch. If this wasn't Dorisca Judice's house, it was that of a very close relative raised with the same taste. It hurt that a woman like that would be driving a beautifully restored 1965 Mustang convertible, the car of my dreams. Which was the reason I noticed her in the first place.

I drove on to the corner of Thirty-fourth Street and stopped, grabbing a grocery-store receipt out of my purse and writing down the number and street name: 1904 Newhope Drive.

I got back to Paw-Paw's shack at a little after four in the afternoon. I'd left Ho baby-sitting when I went for my interview with What a Hoot, but found Pucci there instead. When I walked in the door, Paw-Paw was in the middle of one of my favorite union stories.

"You know what we asking for, Bo?" Paw-Paw asked Pucci.

"No, sir, I don't."

"Hospiddlzation. Everybody has hospiddlzation, yeah Bo? Not us in them refineries right after the war, I tell you what. So we go on strike. And them big boys, them suits, they say, 'No way you comin' back, we gonna get us some scabs,' and damned if they don't, Bo, I tell you what. They brung in two hunnard of the meanest sumbitches you ever seen and you jest know they paying them boys twice what they ever paid us!

"So we stand the pickets ever day, and ever day somebody he get hit upside the head with a baseball bat one of them scabs got. Then some the union boys they get mad. They say, 'Who these scabs what they brung in anyway? That ain't no way to treat a man done gone to war for his country!' And they right, Bo, yeah?"

"Sounds okay by me, Mr. Broussard," Pucci said.

"You call me Tobert, okay, Bo?"

"Sure, Tobert. My name's Sal."

"Now that's a little gal's name, ain't it, Bo?"

"Short for Salvatore, Tobert. It's Italian."

"Okay by me, Bo, even if you peoples was on the wrong side during the Big One.

"Anyways, them union boys they go home they get they guns and they come back and somebody done tipped off the suits and the scabs 'cause we get there to the refinery and damned if they ain't a hunnard scabs and suits and cops all lined up with rifles and the shooting it do commence."

"Wow," Pucci said.

I came in quietly and sat down next to Paw-Paw on the couch, curling up and putting my arm across his scrawny shoulders.

"Well, Bo, we running like the chickens ain't got no heads, I tell you what! My friend Aldus what I served in the Navy with he got a slug in his arm done tore off half his flesh. Lost the use a that arm from then on."

"You're kidding," Pucci said.

"Pas de betises," Paw-Paw said. Pucci looked at me.

"No joking," I translated.

"But then, Bo, listen me tell you. Three day! Three day this go on! Four scab they dead. Two our boy dead. One cop he in the hospiddle. The store they all close up they won't sell us no more ammunition and we 'bout to run out. The suits they holed up in they homes they won't come out they scared shitless, I tell you what. They try get them scabs go home but them boys having too good a time. And they wanna get us for they four dead, yeah?"

Pucci nodded encouragement.

"So the fourth day we heading for the refinery. Them scab boys all lined up they got they guns and they got they bats and they shivs. They gonna get them some union butt, big time. And us, we coming the other way and we got guns and maybe a couple rounds apiece 'cause that's all we got left and things they ain't looking good. Genevieve she say when I leave the house, she say, 'Don't you be leaving me with eight young 'uns to feed ain't got no daddy,' but I gotta go. 'Cause in them days, Bo, the union it bigger than just you paycheck, know what I mean?"

"Yes, sir, I do."

"The union be your brothers and you don't go staying home with the womanfolk when you brothers they gonna fight, you unnerstand, Bo?"

Pucci nodded his head. "Yes, sir, I do."

"So we standing there on either side Beaumont Road, the scabs on one side and us on the other. We yelling fit to beat the band. Them yelling at us and us yelling at them. I was like in the middle of the line and I see the line to the right it be getting quiet. On both side. Them scabs quieting down and my boys quieting down and they all looking toward the right. I look too, Bo, and you know what I seen?"

"No, sir, I surely don't," Pucci said, and I grinned to myself at his word usage. Twenty-four hours in Texas and he was turning into a "bubba."

"They's a man walking down the middle of the road. He got a Remington twelve-gauge in one hand and a Dr Pepper in the other. Wearing a big ole western hat. Boots. Tall boy, mean face. He just walking down the road bigger 'n life."

"Who was he?" Pucci asked.

"Texas Ranger, that who," Paw-Paw said with pride. "They call them up say we got a riot going on in Port Arthur. What they do? They send in one man."

"What happened?" Pucci asked.

"Like I say, he just walking slow down the white line in the middle of the road with that sawed-off throwed back over his shoulder. Wearin' khaki, Ranger badge on his chest, pants got creases in 'em could cut a man in two, big old nickel-plated forty-five on his hip. He din say a word or pay no mind to all the hollerin' and arm waving. When he catch somebody eye, he just nod, no expression, just nod. By the time he get to the end of the row of mens, the line behind him be gone or going. Nobody mess with a Ranger if he be smart."

Paw-Paw shrugged. "After that, the scabs they go home and the union go back to the table with the suits. We finally got us some hospiddlzation but it took another four months. But that's the story of the Port Arthur riot of forty-eight."

Pucci grinned. "The one riot/one Ranger story, I've heard about that but I always thought it was bullshit."

"Ain't no bullshit, Bo. 'S truth."

Paw-Paw got up on his crutches. "I gotta go lay down awhile, *ti-cher*," he said to me. He kissed me on the top of the head. "You be nice to this boy, *ti-cher*, you give him half a chance he listen real good."

Pucci and I watched Paw-Paw make his slow way to the bedroom. Once the door closed behind him, Pucci said, "I see where you get it."

"Get what?" I asked, stretching out on the couch.

"Whatever it is that makes you you," Pucci said. I glanced at him. He was shaking his head. "I don't know—that feisty streak, that . . . strength, I guess."

I sat up. Strength? I was the weakest person I knew. I couldn't walk past a store selling Godiva chocolates without spending my last dime. I fell in love at the drop of a jock-strap. I knew I'd be the one to call Phoebe in the end and apologize. I always did. As usual, Pucci didn't know what the hell he was talking about. I didn't reply. Instead, I pulled the slip of paper with Dorisca Judice's address on it out of my purse and handed it to him.

"What's this?" Pucci asked.

"The address of our number-one suspect."

"Suspect of what?" he asked.

"Are you down here on vacation, Pucci, or are you down here to help me solve a murder?"

"Oh, yeah. Cousin Will's mama. What did you say Cousin Will looked like?"

"I didn't. This woman," I said, pointing at the grocery-store receipt in Pucci's hand, "ran off with Leticia's husband thirty years ago—"

"Good motive—"

"She may not have done it. Probably didn't. My real suspect is Leticia's husband, Armand. But nobody admits to seeing him for fifteen years. I'd bet a bundle Dorisca Judice has."

"Has what?" Pucci said, obviously not paying attention.

"Seen Armand!" I said, grabbing the paper out of his hand. "Jeez, Pucci, pay attention! We can drive by there tomorrow and question her."

He grinned. "Sorry, Kruse. I forgot to bring my bright light and rubber hose with me."

I stood up and headed into the kitchen, mainly to get away from him. There weren't a lot of places to retreat to in Paw-Paw's shack. "There are more subtle ways, Pucci. Let me try to bring you into the twentieth century."

He leaned back in his chair and grinned at me. "While you're doing that, guess who I talked to today?"

I poured myself a glass of water and went back into the living room, resigned that I wasn't getting rid of Pucci any-time soon. "Phoebe," I said.

He shook his head, the grin still holding on. "Nope. Cousin Will."

Oh, God. I sat up straight, trying to imagine what that conversation must have been like.

Pucci: "Hello?"

Will: "Who's this?"

Pucci: "Who's this?"

Will: "I asked you first."

Pucci: "Who do you want to speak to?"

Will: "Is Kimmey there?"

Pucci: "Who wants to know?"

Will: "Who did you say this was?"

Pucci: "Kimmey's . . . friend. From Chicago."

Will: "Kimmey's . . . friend?"

Pucci: "And who's this?"

Will: "Kimmey's other . . . friend."

Pucci: "Oh, the blood relation."

"What did he say?" I asked, trying to get the fantasy out of my mind.

"Wants you to call him," Pucci said, the grin still plastered on his face.

I sighed. "What did you say to him?"

"Say to him?" Pucci was wide-eyed in his innocence.

"Yes, say to him," I said between gritted teeth.

"Nothing! What could I possibly say to him? We've never met!"

I stood up. "Go home. Or at least back to Ho's. I need to make a phone call."

Pucci settled back in his chair, arms behind his head, legs crossed. "I'm comfortable," he said.

"Not for long," I said, heading to the kitchen, where I ran a glass of water, took it back to Pucci's chair and poured it over his head. The pressure of the water moved his slicked-back hair, revealing the reason Pucci wore it that way, showing off his sexy receding hairline—to cover a bald spot in the back. In a few years he'd only have a tuft of hair growing out of the middle of his head.

He yelled and sputtered but got up from the chair.

"Go home," I said.

"You're no fun," Pucci said, heading for the back door,

muttering all the way. "You used to be fun, but you're not fun anymore . . ."

I dried the genuine Naugahyde chair off with a towel and dialed Will's number.

"Who was that man who answered the phone?" Will asked when I had him on the line.

"Ah, a friend of mine from Chicago down here on vacation."

"Oh. I didn't realize . . ." Will said, his voice and his words trailing off.

"Realize what?"

"That you were involved with someone," he finally got out.

"I'm not involved with Pucci!"

"Who?"

"Pucci. That's his name. The man who answered the phone. The man I'm not involved with."

"Then why is he there?"

Why indeed. How in the world was I to explain Pucci to someone as sane as Cousin Will?

"It's a long story. Why did you call?" I asked.

"Well, I wanted to see you, but . . ."

"And I want to see you. Where and when?"

Will laughed. "It's a good thing I like aggressive women," he said. "And there's one aggressive woman in particular I'm quite fond of."

"Who?" I demanded. I'd kill her. Whoever she was.

"You."

I said, "Oh," in my most sheepish manner.

"I'll pick you up tonight. Seven o'clock."

Pick me up. Come in his car. Get out of it. Get met not by me or even Paw-Paw but Pucci. No way in hell.

"I'll meet you. It's such a long drive out here to the bridge. Where?"

"Tony B's? On Fortieth Street? Great Cajun food."

"I'll be there with bells on."

I rang off and ran to get dressed for my date. With my cousin. Oh, well.

Chapter

7

IT WAS ONE OF THOSE MAGICAL SUMMER NIGHTS—THE STARS PEEK-ing through the smog, the fart-and-rotten egg smell of the refineries almost overcome by the smell of new-mown grass and exhaust fumes, the ever-present hum of mosquitoes drowned out by the raucous laughter of drunken teenagers playing chicken on the freeway. I drove to the restaurant where I was to meet Will, glancing at the map of the town on the passenger side seat, and thinking of summer in Austin.

I hadn't been in Austin for more than a day or two since April and missed it. I missed the weekends on the lake with ski boats and sailboats and too much beer. I missed the loud music and good times on the patio of La Zona Rosa, eating jalapeño—everything washed down with quarts of Dos Equis. I missed the sweaty bodies, bad air-conditioning, and great music at Antone's, and dropping pennies on the heads of tourists from the twelfth floor of the Capitol Building. I missed quiet, reflective moments at the Japanese Gardens at

Zilker Park and the cold, cold waters of Barton Springs; I missed the chicken fried steak at Threadgills' and the fish tacos at Ballyhoo's. After three days in the coastal flatlands of Port Arthur, I missed the beauty of the place—the rolling hills and jagged rock cliffs, the huge oak trees and houses teetering off cliffs. And I missed Phoebe. Damn her eyes anyway.

Phoebe and I had not gone a day without talking with each other since the day we met in the seventh grade at Lamar Junior High. No matter where we were, we called. Even when we were mad at each other. I knew I'd call her tomorrow to let her know I got the job at What a Hoot and to tell her I'd be paying her back the thousand shortly. And I knew we'd probably ignore the fact that we'd had words. We usually did. I'm sure most therapists would say that wasn't good—we should communicate our feelings. But Phoebe and I had a long relationship based on each of us stuffing our feelings—a relationship that has lasted longer than either of our marriages or, for that matter, any marriage I knew, other than my parents'—and hers. She'd write her feelings down in her journal and I'd put mine in my act. That's how we dealt with it, how we coped. And it worked for us.

I finally saw Tony B's in a strip shopping center, passed it, made a U-turn, and pulled into the parking lot. Getting out of the car, I wondered if Will would approve of my appearance. For all his greatness, he did seem a little conservative. I had dressed accordingly, in a mid-calf, muslin, tie-dyed skirt in muted shades of orange, pink, and blue, and a white silk, waist-length, double-breasted jacket I'd found in a second-hand shop in Toledo. Under it all, of course, I wore my Bill Blass long johns and had topped the whole ensemble off with a hot-pink baseball cap. What's not to love, right?

I went in and saw him sitting at a table near the front. On seeing me, he smiled and stood. And I got wet all over—

from the palms of my hands to between my toes. He was wearing a summer-weight cream-colored suit with a red T-shirt. His pale skin and black hair sparkled and his blue-blue eyes danced in the light. I walked up to him and he took my hand, bending down to kiss my cheek.

"You look great," he said.

"You, too," I said. I sighed. "How related are we, Will?"

Will laughed. "Third cousins. What they call kissin' cousins. Or second cousins once removed, but I'm not sure about that."

"How does one get removed anyway?"

"That's what I'm not sure of."

We both laughed, both sat, and both took the other's hand. I wondered if he could find work in Austin. I really didn't want to raise the little ones in Port Arthur. Mosquitoes, you know.

"Anyway," he said, rubbing the space between my thumb and index finger with his thumb, "we are not in any way closely related. Hypothetically speaking, our children would have no worries of inbreeding."

"That's nice to know," I said, leaning my head on one hand while the other was busily being caressed. His touch did things to me. Curious things, strange things. Definitely X-rated things.

"You people gonna order?"

The voice sounded so much like Cousin Norvella's, it was enough to ruin anyone's appetite. I glanced up. She was my cousin's clone. The only difference—there were no babies attached to her.

"We need menus," I said.

"Don't got menus, got a blackboard—jeez!" She stormed off.

Will laughed and pointed at a large board behind me. I

wanted to tell the surly waitress she was wrong—it wasn't a black board, it was a green board.

"What do you usually get?" I asked, making sure my hand didn't stray from his.

"The blackened red snapper's good. So's their gumbo."

We discussed the proffered food items for a while and finally settled on our orders. Of course it took twenty minutes for the waitress to come back.

Will ordered a bottle of house white and we sipped while waiting for the food, and talked. His childhood, my childhood. His dreams, my dreams. His past loves, my past loves. All that first-date garbage that goes over much better when you are exceedingly hot for the other person.

We left the restaurant around ten and I followed him to a video-rental store. It was his suggestion that we rent a movie and go back to his apartment. I was vacillating between *Body Heat, Sea of Love,* and *Thief of Hearts,* my three favorite dirty movies, when Will picked out the latest Eddie Murphy. Oh, well. He was probably trying to be sensitive to my profession.

I'd been to his apartment building the day I helped him move his mother's car, but not inside his apartment. It was a roomy two-bedroom with a big-screen TV, furniture that looked rented, and no personality whatsoever. He poured us both a glass of wine and stuck Mr. Murphy in the VCR. Eddie hadn't even begun to run for Congress when Will's hands found my face, turned it to his, and kissed me. A definite curly-toes kiss. His mouth moved to my neck, his hands to my waist, then my butt, then under the white silk jacket. I had my hands under his jacket, removing it from his shoulders. We kissed again. Long and hard. His hand touched my breast.

I pulled back. "I can't do this until I know definitely what 'removed' means," I said.

"What?" He wasn't listening. He pulled me back, lowering me to a lying position on the couch.

I squirmed under him. "No, really, Will. This removed business has me concerned."

"Shh . . ." he said, nuzzling my neck, his right hand going under my skirt.

I jerked away and landed in a heap on the floor. Looking up at Will, I saw him lying on the couch, head propped up on one elbow. "What are you doing, Kimmey?"

"I mean, how do we know removed doesn't make you more related than, say, third cousins?" I said.

"What?"

"If you get removed twice, does that make you first cousins again? What's the legality here?"

He reached down for me. "Kimmey . . ."

I scooted away. "If your mother and my grandmother were first cousins, then that makes us—"

"Third cousins," he said, reaching for me. He fell off the couch. I stood up.

"Except for the removed business. If your grandmother and my grandmother were first cousins, then, sure, okay, maybe we'd be third cousins. But I think the removed thing comes in here with the fact that it was your *mother* and my *grandmother,* don't you see?" I said, heading for my purse and the door. "The problem is the removed business. You understand that, don't you, Will?"

Will was lying on the floor, one arm over his eyes. "I don't understand anything at all, Kimmey."

"Well, you understand that we can't just blatantly go through with this when future generations could be damaged because of it, now can we?"

I didn't wait for an answer. I left.

* * *

I drove back to the bridge wondering what in the hell had happened to me. He was definitely the sexiest man I'd met in months and here I was making excuses not to sleep with him. Okay, in today's climate, indiscriminate sex was not healthy. We really didn't know each other all that well. We were related in some way. And . . .

I pulled over on the oystershell shoulder and pulled on the emergency brake. And Pucci was waiting for me at home. Naw—couldn't be. No way. This had absolutely nothing to do with Pucci. I just needed more time. Okay, granted. I'd gone to bed with men I knew a much shorter time than Cousin Will. I mean Will. And a good high-quality condom helped alleviate some of the worry of AIDS and other nasties. And of course we weren't all that closely related. But it definitely had nothing whatsoever to do with Pucci.

The truth of the matter was I was more serious about Will than other men I'd met over the years. I wanted to get to know him better before bedding him. I wanted him to respect me. It had nothing to do with Pucci. Absolutely nothing.

I took off the parking brake and pulled back onto the road, breathing a sigh of relief.

The next day was Saturday and I had my What a Hoot gig from 8 A.M. to 12 P.M. Another instructor took the afternoon shift. The TEA was very strict about a solid eight hours of defensive driving to remove a blot from one's record, so I left the marina a little after seven, arriving at the strip shopping center housing What a Hoot at a little before seven-thirty. I'd picked out my materials the day before, when I got the job, so all I had to do now was refresh my memory and try to think of something funny to say. I had a file at home of some standards for defensive driving—I'd have to get Phoebe to fax them to me later.

I walked into the classroom at five minutes to eight and was greeted by fifteen people. The entire roster for the day. Or $52.50. Whichever way you want to look at it.

I greeted them with the only line I remembered from my former gig: "The definition of the designated driver is NOT the first one who throws up."

~ By noon, my jaw hurt too much to eat, which for me is really saying something. My standard routine at a club is fifteen minutes to half an hour, depending on whether I'm the opening or middle act. The headliner gets anywhere from an hour to infinity, but since I've never had that designated position, I've never worried about it. Doing four hours with two fifteen-minute breaks was more than rough—it was nigh on impossible. Try smiling and being funny for four hours. It ain't easy, folks. Especially with a sober audience.

As I walked to Paw-Paw's car, I saw a silver Z parked at the other end of the strip-center parking lot. A car identical to Will's. I squinted my eyes and could see a figure sitting on the driver's side, which was the side nearest me. I smiled to myself. Now would be a good time to make amends for the previous night. He must think I'm an idiot. I moved back under the awning of the strip center, walking toward his car. That's when the passenger side door opened and a woman got out. Wearing a floral-patterned sundress, her permed blond hair without the benefit of a big brimmed hat for a change.

I shrank into the shadows of a store doorway. I was close enough to hear her as she said, "It's just not something I want bandied about, Willard . . ."

I could hear Will's voice from the car but could not distinguish the words. "Well, she better not have said anything to anyone, I'm telling you, Willard . . ."

Will responded again and Barbara Sue straightened up, leaning her head toward the sky. "Lord help me," she said. She slammed the door and walked briskly toward a Chevy Blazer parked two spots over.

Will started the engine of the Z and sped out of the parking lot. I waited until Barbara Sue had followed suit, then got in Paw-Paw's Chevy and headed back to the bridge.

Secrets. My family was rife with secrets. The old ones and the young ones. Everybody seemed to have them. "And the truth will set ye free." That's what Cousin Leticia had said shortly before she'd gone to the car for a rest. What truth? Whose truth? Who was the "she" Barbara Sue was referring to? Leticia? Norvella? Me-Maw? Me? Was this what it was always like living this close to family? Was my mother the smart one to get out when she did and to stay as far away as she had? Why was I even here? Getting mixed up in these people's business? Me, the three-times-a-year relative—summer vacation, Christmas, and either Thanksgiving or Easter. But it had been years since I'd even been a three-times-a-year relative. Since turning eighteen, I'd been more an every-few-years relative. I didn't see these people enough to be let in on the secrets, or even to be a part of their everyday lives. I knew they loved me, and I loved them, but did I have any right to delve into their hidden pasts? Would I want them delving into mine?

I got back to Paw-Paw's at about twelve-thirty and walked in the door to the smell of spaghetti and garlic bread. Paw-Paw and Ho were sitting at the dining table, each with a napkin at their chin and forks and big spoons in their hands. Pucci was busy in the kitchen, pouring meat sauce over spaghetti. My jaws suddenly felt better.

"Well, if it's not Kimmey Kruse, back from making the roads safe again," Pucci said, piling plates with fragrant food.

I peeled away to my long johns in honor of the un-air-conditioned shack, sat down next to Paw-Paw and poked a napkin in the bodice of the sleeveless long-john top, holding my fork and spoon high.

Paw-Paw leaned over and whispered in my ear, "*Ti-cher,* you shouldn't be undressing in front of peoples. Give mens bad ideas."

"I'm dressed," I said, indicating the long johns.

"You think you Me-Maw think that dressed?"

Sweat was already pouring down my arms and wetting my hair. "Paw-Paw, just be glad I'm keeping this on, okay?"

"*Gete toi, ti-cher,*" Paw-Paw stage-whispered, which basically meant "Watch out for yourself."

I'm not sure if he was warning me about Me-Maw's wrath or Pucci's lust. I let it pass.

꙰ Pucci helped me wash the dishes while Paw-Paw and Ho played crazy eights.

My hands in soapy water, I said to Pucci, "When we finish with this, you want to go over to Newhope Street?"

"Is it air-conditioned there?" Pucci asked.

"One can only have"—I turned with a flourish—"new hope."

"And people pay you for this?"

"Seriously—"

"I take everything you say seriously, Kruse—"

"We can go over there and ring the doorbell and have a little chat with Dorisca Judice—"

"Who?"

I whirled around with the dishrag and popped him in the face with it (one of my mother's favorite ways to deal with smart talk, an old Cajun remedy). He spit and spattered and said, "Jesus, Kruse! That's disgusting!"

"You two behave, yeah?" Paw-Paw called from the living room.

"Dorisca Judice," I said between clenched teeth, "the woman who ran off with Leticia's husband! God, Pucci, can you stay with the program, please?"

"Not while you're wearing your underwear," he said.

"These are not underwear," I said. "They're a fashion statement."

"Well, you don't want to know what they're saying to me."

"You're right," I said, letting the water out of the sink and handing him the last dish to rinse. "I don't. Are you going with me to Newhope Street, or am I investigating this murder on my own?"

Pucci sighed. "Nobody's even sure there is a murder, Kruse. Except you."

I leaned my butt against the counter and watched Pucci rinse the last dish. "There's a murder all right," I said, crossing my arms across my chest for emphasis. "And I would like very much to know where Cousin Leticia's ex is. Namely Armand. Don't you wonder that?"

Pucci put the last dish in the drainer and yawned. "Not particularly," he said.

 We took Pucci's rental, since it was air-conditioned, and headed out of the marina. Once on Highway 87, Pucci said, "So, how was your date with your cousin last night?"

"How did you know—Paw-Paw."

Pucci grinned. "Your paw-paw and I are quite simpatico, you know, Kruse. He as much as told me I'd make a great grandson-in-law."

"What? You've been seeing my cousin Norvella behind my back?"

"Who's that?"

I forgot he hadn't actually met any other members of the family other than Paw-Paw. "Someone I'd love to introduce you to. You have so much in common. You're both obnoxious assholes."

"I thought only men could be assholes," Pucci said. "At least that's what you told me in Chicago."

"That's true. How about obnoxious cretins?"

"Thank you," Pucci said, "on behalf of your cousin Norberta—"

"Norvella—"

"And all womankind. Speaking of which, do you know why women have more trouble with hemorrhoids than men?" Pucci asked.

"No, and I've been very happy in my ignorance thus far—"

"Because God made man the perfect asshole!" Pucci actually laughed.

We headed out on the Beaumont Highway toward Thirty-fourth Street.

"Speaking of women," Pucci said, "do you know why God invented them?"

I didn't answer.

"Because sheep can't cook." He laughed. "Okay, wait, I've got a million more. Try to control yourself."

"Pucci, when are you going to give this up?"

"Never, Kruse, never. What's the definition of 'gross'?"

I looked out the window at the passing scenery. Unfortunately, there was none.

"When you open your refrigerator and your rump roast farts at you," Pucci said, cracking himself up again.

"I'm glad to see we've regressed to junior high," I said.

"What's black and red and has a hard time getting through a revolving door?"

"Stop it, okay? Please?"

"A nun with a spear through her head."

"Turn on Thirty-fourth! There! Jeez, Pucci! Stop the sophomoric humor and watch where you're going! Go up to Thirty-fifth and go under the highway and make a U-turn."

He followed my instructions, adding, "Why aren't cowboys circumcized?"

We took the Thirty-fifth Street exit and went under the freeway, heading back toward Thirty-fourth. "So they can have someplace to keep their Skoal when they'r eating!" He turned to me and grinned, pulling onto Thirty-fourth. "That's in honor of your Texas heritage, Kruse."

"Thank you ever so much."

"Why did the monkey fall out of the tree?"

I pointed to the Newhope Street sign. "Turn right! Not another word, Pucci, I swear I'll hurt you."

"Because he was dead."

And that was when I shamed myself. I laughed. Pucci pulled into the driveway of 1904 and I was holding my side laughing. I hate Pucci. I really, really do.

Chapter

8

Dorisca Judice opened the door at our ring. Or actually our cow moo. That's what her doorbell did. Mooed like a cow. Which should have prepared me for the rest of the house, if Dorisca's appearance hadn't already given me a clue, but unfortunately it didn't.

Dorisca stood there in full clown makeup, the bleached-blond hair piled high on her head, wearing skintight leopard-skin knee-length pants, a faded black tube top, three-inch heels, and silver-and-torquoise earrings that reached her collarbone.

"I ain't buying nothin'," she said, starting to slam the door.

I put my hand against it. "Dorisca! Wait. I'm Kimmey. We met at the Foret family reunion?"

"Oh?" She squinted at me, obviously too vain to wear glasses. "Oh, yeah. You're that little girl there when Letica she die." She held the door open wide. "Come in, come in!"

She smiled seductively at Pucci. "And who's this you got with you?"

I am a bitch. With a rotten sense of humor. But I do manage to have fun sometimes. "This is my friend Sal from Chicago. I told him all about you and he wanted to meet you, so . . ."

"Well," Dorisca said, smiling brightly and grabbing Pucci's arm. "You come sit here next to Dorisca on the divan, Sal, and tell me all about yourself, hear?"

While Pucci shot me daggers with his eyes, I settled down in a rocking chair and took in my surroundings. Lavender long-shag carpet on the floor. A couch, love seat, and chair all covered in a purple-and-white cabbage-rose design. The wall behind the couch was a mural of naked nymphs cavorting, all done in lavender and white, behind white latticework. A huge bouquet of plastic flowers (purple, lavender, and white) sat atop the white Formica coffee table. The walls without the naked nymphs were painted a lighter lavender and covered with white plastic sconces, knick-knack shelves, and prints of old masters framed in gilt. One wall was nothing but pictures of Dorisca with men.

I got up from my chair and walked over to the wall. "Oh, how interesting," I said. "I love pictures."

Dorisca was torn between her new man and her old ones, but came over to stand with me and stare at her collection. "This here is my first husband," she said, pointing to a picture of a much younger and much prettier Dorisca standing next to a tall, skinny boy with a large Adam's apple. "He died during the Big One," she said, sighing. "Had an accident during basic training. But I still got my widow's pension, just like he died in the war.

"This one," she said, pointing to a heavily made up but younger Dorisca standing next to an absolutely gorgeous man who had a striking resemblance to Cousin Will, "was Leticia's husband. She always said I took him away from her, but that weren't the truth."

"No?" I asked, trying to keep the flow going.

"No way. He was a frisky one. Ran around with all the girls. Me and him just had a fling for a little while, then he went on home to Leticia. I don't mess with married men all that much." She touched her hair and turned to look at Pucci. "With all I got, it just ain't fair to the wives," she said, smiling at her new find.

Pucci's response of a weak smile and a complexion turning a lovely shade of puce brought a smile and a sigh to my lips. Revenge is sweet, and this was like a hot-fudge-brownie sundae with three flavors of ice cream, whipped cream, sprinkles, and a cherry on top.

Turning back to the business at hand, I asked Dorisca, "So, when was the last time you saw Armand?"

Playing with her hair and staring off into space, she said, "Oo, I dunno. While back. He come by ever so often but not so much since I move to Port Arthur from Armentine."

"How long ago was that? When you moved to Port Arthur?" At this point, I noticed the space she was staring into was occupied by Pucci.

"Do what?" she said.

"When you moved to Port Arthur?" I was beginning to think bringing the distraction of Pucci had been a mistake. I moved, placing myself between the two of them.

Slowly her myopic eyes focused on me. "Oo, I dunno. While back. Maybe twenty year."

"So you haven't heard from Armand in twenty years?"

She moved, trying to remove me as an obstacle for her eye contact with poor Pucci. "Maybe a little more than that," she said, smiling seductively at the poor bugger sitting uncomfortably on the sofa.

"Has he called you, anything like that? You see," I said, moving in front of her again, "the family would like to try to find him. Let him know about Leticia."

"Why for?" she said, focusing on me again. "He don' care none for her alive, why he care she dead?" Her eyes narrowed. " 'Less she left him some little something?"

"No, nothing like that. But he is Will's father and Will wants to find him and let him know," I lied.

She shrugged and moved away from me, planting herself next to Pucci on the couch, her arm looped through his, valiantly tugging him toward her as he ineffectually tried to get away. I knew I was going to pay for this. And I was going to pay big.

"Well," I said, sitting down again in the rocking chair, "you know anyone who might know where he is?"

"Enic might know," Dorisca said, touching one clawlike fingernail to Pucci's cheek. He flinched.

"Enic? The man you were with at the reunion?"

"Oh, I wasn't *with* him," she said, emphasizing the word "with" and winking knowingly at me. "He just be a . . . friend," she said.

"Why would Enic know?" I asked. "Were they friends?"

Dorisca laughed. "Oh, no. Armand he don't have no men friends, yeah? He go after too many wives for mens to be his friends. No, Enic he Armand's cousin. They mothers sisters. Armand, he get his looks from his daddy, that why he so *jolle* and Enic he so pug-ugly."

"Enic lives in Armentine?" I asked.

"Oh, yeah. That boy ain't ever had a lick of ambition. Still live in the house his daddy born in. Drove a truck for the refinery for near forty year and now he retired just go fishing ever day like he some old coon-ass, which just what he is, yeah?"

"So you think Enic might know where Armand is now?"

Dorisca pressed her drooping right breast against Pucci's left arm. "Probable not. But it don't hurt to ask."

"That's true," I said, settling back in my rocking chair and grinning at Pucci.

He stood, almost knocking Dorisca off the couch. "Well," he said, smiling weakly, "we don't mean to keep you, Mrs. Judice—"

Dorisca stood and draped herself over Pucci. "Honey, you can keep me any ole time . . ."

But Pucci wasn't listening. He was out the door, leaving a smitten Dorisca Judice quivering, trembling, and pulsating in his wake.

⁂ "When you least expect it," Pucci said. "Scorpions in your bed late at night. Pig's liver in your shoes. Not to mention writing your home phone number in every biker-bar bathroom in the Greater Chicago area!"

"Sal, honey, you seem upset," I said, patting his knee where it quivered, trembled, and pulsated on the accelerator of his rental car.

"Upset? Kruse, you're a class-act bitch, you know that?"

I smiled sweetly. "Practice, Pucci, practice."

We rode for a while in smoldering silence, punctuated only by my occasional giggle. Finally, I sighed and said, "Well, we got a little something out of her, I suppose. Other than her bra size and position preference."

He glared at me and I giggled again. I have to admit I hadn't had quite this much fun since, as Paw-Paw was fond of saying, the hogs ate my little brother. It's only a saying. I never had a little brother and we never kept hogs. But it's the thought that counts.

"Okay," I started again, trying to get back to business, "we have one other avenue to Armand DuBois. Namely his cousin, the renowned Enic."

"And how are we to find this Enic? Go to Armageddon?"

I laughed. "She really did get to you, didn't she? It's Armentine."

"Whatever. Go there and yell, 'Oh, Enic?' You didn't get his last name, smart-ass."

"Well, Armentine is small enough that it might work. But I was thinking of going to Me-Maw's and asking her Enic's last name and then getting on old Ma Bell."

"They have telephone service in a place called Armentine?" Pucci said.

"It's quite possible," I said. I caught his eye and grinned. He glared at me.

We pulled into the driveway at Me-Maw's house. She came flying out the door to greet me, but stopped dead when she saw Pucci.

"Me-Maw," I said, indicating the Italian stallion, "this is Sal Pucci, my friend from Chicago. Sal, this is my grandmother, Mrs. Broussard."

Me-Maw stuck her hand out like a trooper and shook Pucci's. "How you do?" she said.

"Fine, Mrs. Broussard," Pucci said, all formality. "How are you?"

"Well, I got a spot of neuralgia," she said, moving her hand to the middle of her back, "and my sinuses been actin' up something fierce."

I took Me-Maw's arm and walked her toward the door. "Me-Maw, can we get some iced tea, maybe? And I need to use the phone."

"Oo-eee, where my manners? Girl, you bring your young

man on in the house I get you both something to eat. Mr. Sal, you like Cajun food?"

Pucci followed us in the house. "Yes, ma'am. I certainly do."

"Well, I got some leftover crawfish bisque and some okra gumbo. That do you?"

Pucci was all grins as he followed Me-Maw into the kitchen.

"Me-Maw," I said, sitting down at the kitchen table, "I need to get ahold of Enic. That man who was with Dorisca Judice at the reunion?"

"Why for you want to talk to ole Enic? He dumber than dirt, girl, that's a fact."

"Well, I need to talk to him because I understand that he's Armand DuBois's cousin."

Me-Maw gave me the old fish eye. "So?"

"So I'd sorta like to know where old Armand is, Me-Maw."

"You still going on about poor Leticia, God rest her soul"—Me-Maw crossed herself—"being murdered, girl?"

"Me-Maw, I think it's a great possibility."

"Nobody wanna hurt poor Leticia," she said, putting bisque and gumbo in the microwave. "And if they do, girl, you stay out of it. You don' wanna go messing with things like that. And wherever Armand DuBois be he best stay there."

"That's why Sal's here, Me-Maw. He's a policeman."

Me-Maw turned and looked at Pucci. Most Cajuns are very law-abiding citizens and Me-Maw has got to be one of the most law-abiding. But there's this genetic thing from the bayou. Once a suppressed minority, always a suppressed minority. The distrust was in her eyes.

"Enic, his last name Hebert." She reached in her what-not drawer and pulled out an old red leatherette address book and read off Enic's home phone number. I scribbled it hastily on a scrap of paper from my purse and went down the hall to the phone, leaving Pucci alone once again with a predatory Cajun female.

 "Armand DuBois?" Enic said after I'd introduced myself and reminded him of our connection. "Lord, ain't heard that name in a month of Sundays. I tell you, *cher,* I ain't seen nor heard a Cousin Armand in, Lord Awmighty, twenty, thirty year. All his kinfolk be long gone and I knowed about his wife, Leticia. Well, you was there, girl . . ."

"Yes, sir. That's why we're trying to reach Armand. To let him know about Leticia."

"She leave him something?" Enic asked and I could smell the greed over the wire.

"No. It's just that Will would like his father to know, that's all," I said, using the same lie I'd told Dorisca. No reason to tell more lies than absolutely necessary. It's hard to keep them straight when you do. "Do you know about any of his, well, women friends?"

Enic hooted laughter from his end of the phone line. "How much time you got, *cher?* That boy always got him some ladies, and he don' share none, let me tell you what."

"Can you think of any woman in particular, other than Dorisca, of course."

"Well, there was that Covet girl from Alexandria, but she died a while back, I heard. Oh, and there was the Foret girl."

I stiffened all over. "Foret girl? Which Foret girl?"

Unfortunately, Enic heard the stiffness of my voice. "Who you say you was?" he asked. "Who you kin to?"

I sighed. "I'm Genevieve Broussard's granddaughter."

"Oh." There was silence on the line for almost a full minute. "Look, *cher,* I don't be talkin' out of school about nobody, yeah? Armand he a bad ass, ain't no two ways about it.

And I ain't heard from him nor seen him in years. So that's all I can tell you, yeah?" And he hung up.

I sat there on the hall floor, stunned. "One of the Foret girls." Foret was a common-enough name in Louisiana, granted. But when he realized my relationship to Me-Maw, he hushed up big time. Which meant that the Foret girl he was speaking of was of one particular Foret family. And that one particular Foret family was mine. Me-Maw and her four sisters.

The phone rang before I'd had a chance to get up off the floor. I picked it up as if I lived there.

"Mrs. Broussard's residence," I said, just as Me-Maw had taught me that summer years before when she'd let me answer the phone for the first time all by myself. I believe I was twelve. Me-Maw never was one for indulging children.

The voice in my ear said, "I looking for Mrs. Broussard's granddaughter, name of Kimberly, I do believe."

"This is she speaking," I said, wondering who this was on the other end of the line.

"Well, this is Dorisca Judice what you come to see a while ago?"

"Ah, yes, Mrs. Judice. Can I help you?"

"I got me a friend on the Port Arthur Po-lice Department who come see me a little while ago and I tell him 'bout you coming to visit and about old Leticia and he say you come up to the po-lice department and you say you think Leticia she murdered, yeah? You say that, girl?"

I sat on the floor wishing I were home in Austin, curled up on my genuine Hollywood bed with my one-eyed flea-bitten cat curled up in my lap. Or even back at Chez Butch having my hair butchered. Anything but sitting in the hallway of my me-maw's house worrying about Foret girls and having to deal with Dorisca Judice. Mine was not a fair life. It really wasn't.

"Well, Mrs. Judice, I did sorta mention that, yes, ma'am."

"Why you think that, girl?"

"Ah, well, it has to do with dead wasps."

"Uh-huh."

"It's sorta complicated, Mrs. Judice," I said.

"I ain't stupid, girl. Tell me," she said.

"Why?" I countered.

"Curious," she said.

"Well," I said, not being in the mood to deal with curious, horny old ladies, "I'm in the middle of something right now, Mrs. Judice. May I call you back?"

"Well, sure," she said, "let me give you the number."

I listened to her recite her telephone number, not bothering to write it down. All I could think of was Armand DuBois and his Foret girl.

I drove Pucci's rental back to the bridge. He sprawled beside me, occasionally suppressing a belch. "If you could cook like that, I'd marry you," he finally said.

"Good enough reason never to learn," I shot back.

I could feel his eyes on me as I drove, keeping mine straight ahead on the narrow island road. "What's eating you, Kruse? I thought that little debacle with the delectable Dorisca would keep you in grins for a week."

"Nothing," I said, swerving to miss a possum moving across the road in the dusky evening light.

"What did old Enic have to say?" Pucci asked.

"Nothing!" I said. Too emphatically.

Pucci sat up. I know it took a great deal for him to do that, but I still wasn't all that impressed.

"I thought we were partners on this, Kruse."

I didn't say anything.

"It's not fair to keep information from your partner, Kruse."

I still didn't say anything.

"What did Enic tell you?"

I pulled the car over on the soft shoulder and shut off the engine. We sat there quietly for a moment. Mosquitoes buzzed at the closed windows and swam around the bug carcasses on the windshield. Pucci didn't ask any more questions. He knew I was going to tell him and he was giving me the space to do it. It didn't endear him to me. Very little has.

"One of Armand's women was one of my great-aunts. Or my grandmother," I finally said.

Pucci burst into laughter. Which stopped when I almost slapped him in the face. If my reflexes had been better and his worse, the contact would have been mind-boggling. As it was, he held my wrist in his grip and said, "I'm sorry. You're right to be angry. Tell me."

He let go of my arm and I settled back in the seat, cracking a window for some air and hoping the mosquitoes couldn't find it. They did. "There were five of them—the Foret girls. Me-Maw, my Aunt Adele, Aunt Blanche, Aunt Laurina, and Clothilde. Clothilde died when she was a child. Flu, I think. Aunt Blanche died before I was born. In childbirth. The baby was stillborn, and as the story goes, her husband ran off in grief to the bayou and was eaten by an alligator."

"You're shitting me," Pucci said.

"That's the story. Not a new one around here. People do get eaten by alligators, you know."

"Actually, no, I didn't know."

"Anyway, that leaves only Laurina, Adele, and Genevieve, my grandmother."

"Adele is the one you went to the reunion with, right?"

"Right. She lives here in Port Arthur. Aunt Laurina lives in Orange and she was at the reunion, too. Along with four of her eight children and a plethora of grandchildren and great-grandchildren."

"So you think one of these old ladies was a main squeeze of the great Armand."

I turned and glared at him. "No. I don't. I think Enic heard a nasty rumor. That's what I think."

Pucci's hand touched my cheek. "This isn't so much fun anymore, is it, babe?"

"Pucci—"

That's all I got out before his lips were on mine. And, Lord, can that man kiss.

Chapter

9

"TONGUE?" PHOEBE ASKED.

"No tongue."

"Openmouthed or closed?"

"Open," I replied.

"You or him?"

"Both."

"How long?" she asked.

"No more than a minute."

"A full minute?"

"Maybe a little less."

I left out the lip-nibbling. I don't tell Phoebe *everything*.

I was lying on the couch at Paw-Paw's, my grandfather tucked away for the night and Pucci safely ensconced in Ho's Scenic Cruiser. It was after midnight and it was quite necessary that I discuss the kiss with Phoebe. She is a world-class kiss analyzer. Not so much for those she receives personally, but for others.

"Okay," she said, ready to give her studied opinion, "almost a full minute with mouths open—"

"Just a little—"

"Mouths open just a little and no tongue. Did he try?"

"What? To give me the tongue?"

"Right."

"Not to my knowledge."

"You'd know," she said. "Okay. He's serious about you."

"Jesus! Phoebe, give me a break!"

"The man, I believe, is in love," she declared.

"No way," I said, my denial a thing of actual beauty.

"Listen. No tongue even though your mouth was open: Respect. His mouth open and still no tongue: Respect mixed with suppressed passion. This is serious stuff."

"The suppressed passion I'll buy," I said.

"What happened afterward? After the kiss? Who pulled away first?"

I thought about it. Something I'd been doing steadily since it had happened. Did I dare tell her the parting was mutual and that we sat for another full minute, our foreheads touching and not saying a word? She'd be buying my trousseau. I was the first to pull away from that and started the car, driving us straight to Paw-Paw's. Pucci and I hadn't said a word to each other. He came in the house, said hi to Paw-Paw, then excused himself for Ho's. It was barely nine o'clock. Was this a serious turning point in our relationship? Were we no longer bickering friends? Were we lovers-to-be? Then what about Cousin Will? I mean, Will?

To get off the sticky subject of my love life, I told Phoebe about the even stickier possible love life of one of the Foret "girls" and the Great Armand DuBois.

"So ask your grandmother," the greatest deposition-taker in Austin said.

"Oh, right. Mrs. Broussard, are you or any of your sisters

now or have you ever been adulterously involved with Armand DuBois?"

"What would she say?" Phoebe asked.

"She'd wash my mouth out with soap."

"So? One of your aunts?"

I thought about it. Possibly Adele. She and I got along fairly well. I'd barely spoken to Aunt Laurina at the reunion, no more than "Yes, ma'am, you're right. I haven't grown much."

Tomorrow was Sunday and I'd promised to go to mass with Me-Maw. Aunt Adele would more than likely be there, but there wouldn't be much time to talk without Me-Maw present. And Ho had said—or rather, Paw-Paw had told me that Ho had said—he wasn't going to be around much on Sunday because that was the day he visited his married son in Beaumont, so I'd have to do most of the Paw-Paw sitting after mass. Tuesday night I had my next gig at What a Hoot, but that was in the evening. I'd find a way. I had to.

I was in the bathroom the next morning when the phone rang. I heard Paw-Paw pick it up. Through the shack's thin walls, I could hear his every word.

"Hello? . . . uh-huh . . . uh-huh . . . uh-huh . . . uh-huh . . . uh-huh . . . jes' a minute. Kimberly!"

I flushed and came out of the bathroom. "It's you Me-Maw," he said, handing me the phone.

I took the receiver from him and said, "Hey, Me-Maw."

"That man!" she said. "He giving you grief, girl?"

"No, ma'am."

"Well, don' you let him give you no grief. That all that man know how to do—give womens grief."

"He's been fine, Me-Maw," I said.

"You comin' mass this morning?" she asked.

"Yes, ma'am. What time?"

"You be there at ten-thirty, girl. You hear me?"

"Yes, ma'am. I'll be there."

I hung up and looked at my Spiro Agnew watch. It was nine o'clock. It took half an hour to drive from the bridge to the church. My makeup was on, my hair, such as it was, fixed, all I had to do was put on some clothes suitable for mass. It would have been easy if I owned any.

Paw-Paw was sitting on the sofa, his casted leg propped on a pillow on the coffee table, the Sunday *Port Arthur News* in front of his face.

"Paw-Paw," I said.

He put down the paper and looked at me. *"Oui?"*

"I'm going to mass with Me-Maw. You gonna be okay?"

He put the paper back up in front of his face. "Don' worry 'bout me. I be fine. None a you womens need to worry 'bout me. I can take care of my own self—been doing it for thirty-five year! Think I can handle it for another hour or two!"

I sat down next to him on the sofa, gently moving the paper away from his face. "Paw-Paw—"

He leaned his head back on the sofa. "Ever tell you 'bout the time I met you Me-Maw?"

"No, I don't think so," I said.

"A church dance in Sulphur. I go with my friend Bernard 'cause he sweet on this gal gonna be there. I just sitting there minding my own when in walks this big ole gal from Armentine. I walk up and I say, 'Hey, girl, you wanna dance with me?' and she say, 'Boy, you so short I step on you.' "

Paw-Paw laughed. Then he looked at me and shook the paper out, raising it to his face. "Shoulda knowed right then she was gonna be a pain in the ass."

* * *

Me-Maw and Aunt Adele were standing by the front doors of the church when I pulled up in Paw-Paw's Chevy. Me-Maw was looking stern and Aunt Adele was looking concerned. I almost put the car in reverse but I knew they'd seen me. I got out and walked up to the church steps.

"Hey, Me-Maw, Aunt Adele," I said.

"Hey, Kimberly," Aunt Adele said. She looked at Me-Maw. "I go on in now, Genevieve," she said, turning and walking into the church.

Me-Maw cleared her throat. "Girl, we gotta talk," she said. She marched down the steps, passed me, and walked over to the shade of a huge flowering mimosa. She stood there, her arms crossed over her ample bosom.

I sighed and joined her under the tree. "Yes, ma'am?" I said.

"You mama should be the one talking at you about this, girl, not me. Not my place. But you mama off gallivanting around God knows where—"

"Antarctica—"

"Whatever—" She waved my answer away with her hand. She cleared her throat again. "Girl, this boy you brung over to the house. This Mr. Sal. This the boy called you on the telephone?"

Whoa, boy. "Yes, ma'am."

"You be sweet with this boy?"

I cleared my own throat. "He's just a friend," I said.

"You cousin Will he know about this boy?"

"Ah, yes, ma'am."

"Uh-huh. You cousin Will—you be sweet on him?"

"Me-Maw, really, I don't think—"

"I saying this, girl, because you can't be messing with two boy. It ain't right and it be dangerous. So, I just warning you you gotta tell them boys what going on with you so they understand."

"Yes, ma'am," I said, staring off into space. I was twenty-nine years old and have been balancing men for a great number of years. All right, agreed, this one was getting sticky, but I didn't need my seventy-eight-year-old grandmother lecturing me on juggling men.

"Two boy interested the same girl, somebody gonna get killed, *cher,* you unnerstand?"

"Me-Maw, nothing like that's going to—"

Me-Maw put her heavy hand on the top of my head and shook me to my toes. "Listen at me, girl. I know what I be talking about."

I looked up into a face with big brown Cajun eyes, wrinkles whitened by face powder, and liver spots, framed by overly permed gray hair. She folded her arms across her chest again and said, "I be young once, Kimberly Anne. I know how it is. I be going with another boy when you Paw-Paw he come courting. This other boy, Galbert, he a big ole boy out of the bayou, they grows 'em big in the bayou, *cher,* but I could see Galbert he wasn't gonna amount to nothing. All he wants to do all day long is go fishing or hunting with his friends. Then come courting on me at night. But Tobert, he have a job. Worked in the refinery and made good money. I decide I start going out with Tobert, but Galbert he don't take to that none. So he challenge Tobert. And Tobert he say, 'You don' need no knives and no guns. I beat you with my own two hands.' "

Me-Maw was staring off into space, in her memories. I leaned against the tree and listened.

"Well, Galbert he a big boy, like I say. Six foot five inch and almost three hundred pound, and he laughs at little bitty old Tobert and say, 'You come on boy, I whip up the ground with you.' I couldn't go watch, of course, 'cause ladies didn't do that, but your Uncle Lester he was courting your Aunt Adele then and he go watch. He say that Tobert little but he mean and he near bit off Galbert's ear and hit him in places where women don't talk about and ole Galbert he go back into the bayou to lick his wounds."

She stopped. "And what happened?" I asked.

She looked at me like I was crazy. "I married you Paw-Paw, of course. He won me fair and square."

"Oh," I said, wanting to debate the issue of a man actually being able to "win" a woman, but I doubted seriously if Me-Maw had ever heard of the Equal Rights Amendment.

"What I saying, girl, is this: You be careful else one of them boys is gonna get kilt and that won't sit kindly on your mind." Again, she looked off into space. "Always did wonder what ever become of Galbert."

I touched Me-Maw's arm. "Don't worry," I said. "I have everything under control."

"Ha!" she said and strode off. Considering how muddled my mind was at the moment, I think she may have had a point.

   Norvella and her brood were sitting in the same pew as Me-Maw, Aunt Adele, and I. I noticed her husband was no-where to be seen. Smart man.

After church, against my better judgment and to the detriment of my eardrums, I pulled Norvella aside while Me-Maw and Aunt Adele went gaga over Norvella's nasty offspring.

"I saw Barbara Sue the other day," I said.

"Uh-huh," Norvella answered, popping gum and scratching her hip. She was wearing a puce-and-green halter-top dress as a jumper with a white blouse underneath it. The dress was two sizes too small and the shirt appeared to be at least one size too large. And she had the audacity to talk about my hair!

"She and Willard were talking. I thought Willard really

didn't know anybody in the family, since his mother and Me-Maw had been estranged—"

"Oh, we all know Willard," she said, her voice loud enough to be heard at the Methodist Church two miles away.

"At least, me and Barbara Sue knew him 'cause Barbara Sue went to college with him. At Lamar?"

"Oh," I said.

"They were a hot item for a little while," Norvella said and winked.

"Will and Barbara Sue?"

"Oh, yeah. They were sorta engaged 'fore Barbara Sue ran off with that other boy."

"Oh," I said. Interesting.

Secrets. Barbara Sue and Will and Armand Dubois and the Foret girls. Now I knew Barbara Sue's and Will's secret. All that was left was the secret of the Foret girls. And I was bound and determined to find that one out.

"So why can't I go with you?" Pucci asked.

"Because Aunt Adele wouldn't say a word in front of you, that's why," I explained, slamming the door of his air-conditioned rental.

He motioned for me to roll the window down. Grudgingly I did. "Well, okay," he said. "I'll wait here."

"I don't really care where you wait, Pucci."

"You have my car."

"Drive Paw-Paw's if you wanna go someplace."

"Maybe I will. Maybe I'll go into town and have a talk with a certain cousin of a certain someone."

I smiled. It was Monday morning. "He's at work," I said.

I started the car and drove off. Tensions had been running high between Pucci and me since Saturday evening. When I'd gotten back from mass Sunday afternoon, he was playing cards with Paw-Paw, but he left only minutes after I arrived. We barely spoke. That evening, he came over for dinner. A very quiet dinner. While we cleaned up and Paw-Paw was watching "Sixty Minutes," I told Pucci I'd be going to see Aunt Adele the next day. He'd barely nodded. But the next morning, when I'd gone out to get in Paw-Paw's Chevy, Pucci had shown up with the keys to the rental. That conversation was the most we'd spoken to each other since The Kiss.

It took less than thirty minutes in the light morning traffic to get to Aunt Adele's house in the Groves. It was a white clapboard affair with a freshly painted red front door, screened-in side porch, and two pecan trees, whitewashed halfway up. I went to the side porch and inside the screened-in area, knocking on the back door. The front door was only used for funerals and insurance salesmen.

Aunt Adele greeted me in her apron, wiping her flour-coated hands as she opened the back door.

"Oo-eee, Kimberly Anne, what you doing here?"

I smiled. "Just came by to see you, Aunt Adele. Is that okay?"

"You get yourself on in here, girl," she said, shooing me inside.

The kitchen smelled of baking bread, cinnamon, and cloves. I idly wondered how soon whatever was in the oven would be coming out. Breakfast had been at least half an hour before.

The kitchen sparkled, just like the one at Me-Maw's house. The old linoleum was so shiny you could see your reflection in it, and every appliance looked as if it had just come off the showroom floor—circa 1952.

"Sit youself down. I got some spice bread coming out the oven in just a few minutes, you put some May-haw jelly on that, you can die and go to heaven, I tell you what!"

"Sounds great," I said, sitting down while she brought me a cup of Seaport, heavy French-roast coffee, a bowl of sugar, and a cream pitcher. I doctored the coffee and sipped. It was like syrup going down. Not totally bad.

"What bring you here, Kimberly? Not that I mind a visit. I don' get near 'nuff visitors. Who wants to come see an old lady don' got nothing interesting to say, yeah?"

"Well, I just thought I'd drop by—"

"You remember Mrs. Watson what taught you mama in the first grade, I think it was? She had a brain tumor size of a Valley grapefruit. They took it out, she be a vegetable! Educated lady like that! Go figure."

"Um," I said, "a shame."

"And Rose Theriot—"

"Yes, Me-Maw mentioned Mrs. Theriot—"

"Womb just plumb dropped out!"

I shook my head. "That's what Me-Maw told me."

"You remember you uncle Earl Combs what married you cousin Norvella's daddy's mama after her first husband died?"

"Ah—"

"Dead." She looked at me. Hands in her lap, stern look on her face.

"Oh, that's awful," I said, having no idea whom she was talking about. I assumed Norvella's step-grandfather on her father's side, which would be no relation to me whatsoever, and whom I doubt seriously I'd ever met.

Aunt Adele snapped her fingers. "Went just like that." She looked around to make sure no one was listening. As we were the only people in the house, I figured she was safe. "Died on the toilet. Just like Elvis Presley."

I was saved from a response by the bell on the oven. Aunt Adele jumped up and put on an oven mitt, shaped and printed to look like a crawfish. It was so ugly I knew I had to have one just like it. Maybe get some heavy twine and run it through the top as a strap and use it as a purse. God, would that be cool or what?

She talked all the time she was preparing the bread, although I must admit I didn't hear much over all the salivating I was doing. It can get noisy.

She set the bread, butter, and homemade May-haw jelly down in front of us and poured two more cups of coffee.

I cleared my throat, ready with my prepared gambit. "Aunt Adele," I said, my voice pitched a little too high. I cleared my throat again. "Aunt Adele. About Leticia—"

"Oo-eee, wasn't that the most awfullest thing? Such a sweet woman and her and Genevieve finally getting back together after all those years!" She went "tsk, tsk." "God works in mysterious ways, Kimberly Anne, I tell you what!"

"That's true," I said. "I was wondering about Cousin Leticia's husband—"

"Oo-eee, that one! Bad! Not a good bone in his whole body. Too *jolle!*"

"I've been wondering, though, Aunt Adele," I said, picking off pieces of my second thick slice of spice bread liberally smeared with butter and May-haw jelly and stuffing them daintily into my mouth, "where he might be. Armand, I mean."

"Who care! I hope he dead," Aunt Adele said, standing and going for the coffeepot.

"Ah, Aunt Adele. I heard something—"

She jerked around. "The doorbell?"

"Ah, no. I mean, I heard a story and I thought that maybe, if it would be okay, maybe you could tell me what it means, I mean if—"

"Spit it out, girl." She sat back down.

I sighed. This was harder than I'd previously thought. And I'd previously thought it was gonna be damned hard. "I know there's been a lot of talk about Armand and his womanizing."

"Oo-eee, that's the truth."

"I heard . . . well . . . what I heard was that maybe one of the women he had something going with, or maybe someone he just dated, or whatever, well . . . anyway, I heard that one of his women was a Foret girl."

The silence was deafening. Aunt Adele had her coffee cup halfway to her mouth when I let go with my bombshell. For several seconds, it stayed there. Unmoving. The electric clock over the kitchen counter, silent until that moment, ticktocked so loudly it felt like a pulse. Slowly Aunt Adele set the coffee cup down. Her eyes went to the cup and stayed there.

"You go on back to you Paw-Paw's now, Kimberly Anne."

"Aunt Adele—"

She stood up and walked to the doorway separating the kitchen and living room. "Go on, girl," she said, her back to me.

"Aunt Adele, I just heard that. I know it probably isn't true, it's just that—"

She swung around, her face hard. "Get out of my house, Kimberly Anne. You get out right now."

Chapter

10

I GOT BACK INTO PUCCI'S RENTAL AND STARTED IT, TURNING ON the air-conditioning. It was getting close to noon and the heat and humidity were enough to suck the juice right out of you. Not that I noticed. I sat in the car, stunned. My aunt Adele had told me to get out. It doesn't matter how grown up you are, when an older relative talks to you like Aunt Adele had talked to me, it takes you right back to age seven, caught playing doctor with the boy next door. My hands shook on the steering wheel and my throat had that big old bump in it that let me know if I didn't do something quick I was going to burst into tears.

I put the car into gear and drove to Me-Maw's house. Her car was in the driveway, but no one answered my knock on the front door. I went around to the back door and knocked. Still no answer. Peeking in, I saw Me-Maw sitting at the kitchen table, a cup of coffee in her hands, staring at the wall in front of her, her back to me. I knocked again louder and called her name. She didn't move a muscle.

"Me-Maw, please!" I wailed. "Let me in. Please."

There was no movement from the woman who used to think I was pretty hot stuff. Until I mentioned the Foret girls and Armand DuBois.

Feeling like a pound puppy just passed up for the hundredth time, I hung my head and went back to the car.

It was as I pulled off the highway to the marina that my internal dialogue went from "poor baby" to severely pissed.

Who the hell do these old biddies think they are? I asked myself. Treating me like this! What in the hell's going on?

I hit the accelerator and sped to Paw-Paw's shack, pulling into the oystershell drive so fast I skidded into the peacock-shitted yard. I jumped out of the car and ran into the house. Pucci and Paw-Paw were at the kitchen table, Paw-Paw's leg propped up on one of the unused chairs, both well into a game of crazy eights.

"Paw-Paw!" I said.

He turned and looked at me. His eyes narrowed. "What's with you, girl? You look like you seen a ghost."

"Why is it that mentioning a rumor that Armand DuBois may have had a fling with one of the Foret girls has turned both Me-Maw and Aunt Adele to stone?"

Which is almost exactly what the question did to Paw-Paw. His face hardened. He reached for his crutches, got himself to his feet, and started walking to the bedroom.

I grabbed his arm. "Paw-Paw, talk to me! What is going on?"

He twisted out of my grasp. "Girl, I don't gotta tell you nothing," he said. "But I do tell you this one thing—you pack up you bags now and you get the hell outta Port Arthur. And you don't never mention this to you Me-Maw or anybody else ever again, you hear me, girl?"

"I'm not leaving, Paw-Paw. I'm not."

He went into the bedroom and slammed the door.

☙ And he didn't come out, even for dinner. When he wouldn't open the door for me when I offered him dinner on a tray, I sent Pucci. He opened the door for him but didn't say a word.

Pucci was like a rock. But a different kind of rock from the one I seemed to be turning my family into. Pucci was something solid I could lean on. He didn't hate me. The only person in the Greater Port Arthur area who didn't, as far as I could tell. We talked little about Armand DuBois, since there was nothing really to talk about. Pucci left around ten for Ho's place and I showered and slipped under the sheet on the couch.

I'm not sure how late it was when the whispering woke me up. From the moonlight spilling through the open windows I could see Paw-Paw on the phone by the front door. He was whispering. But I could hear most of it.

"Genevieve, it ain't right . . . gotta tell her . . . how long you think you can keep this secret? . . . Don't tell me . . . okay, okay. It's you business. You family, but Genevieve . . . no, honey, now you listen . . . I can call you honey if I want to—you still my wife. Don't start with me . . . the girl don' mean no harm . . . she you grandbaby, Genevieve . . . she don't know what she doin', grant you, but . . ."

He glanced over at me and I slammed my eyes shut, trying to breathe regularly so he'd think I was still asleep.

He turned back to the phone, huddled on his crutches, his shoulders hunched. "Genevieve, you don' tell her I gonna . . . don't tell me . . . okay, okay."

He replaced the receiver gently in the cradle and hobbled back to bed. As he shut the door to his room, I opened my eyes and stared at the ceiling, wondering just what can of worms I'd opened up.

The smell of frying bacon brought Paw-Paw out of his room the next morning. He greeted me as if there'd been no words between us the night before. Of course, I wasn't stupid enough to mention the names Foret or DuBois.

"Gotta doctor's appointment today," Paw-Paw said between mouthfuls of eggs and bacon.

"What time?" I asked.

"Don' worry. Ho takin' me."

"Paw-Paw, that's what I'm here for! To take care of you and take you to the doctor—"

"I ain' no baby, *cher*. 'Sides, me and Ho got some talkin' to do and places to go." Paw-Paw grinned at me, the perfect upper plate slipping just a bit at his large grin. "Ho got the sweets on for this ole gal work for the doctor. Ole coon-ass gal. I tell Ho them coon-ass don' take none to his kind, but he sweet on her jest the same."

I laughed. "Like you're not an old coon-ass," I said.

He feigned indignation and popped my butt as I moved past him with more toast. "Who you callin' a coon-ass, *cher*? Remember what you be half of, now!"

We both laughed. Somehow, the entire exchange smacked of trying just a little too hard. The words from the night before were going to hang heavy for a long time. The words between my grandfather and myself, the words spoken to me by my aunt Adele, and the words not spoken at all by my grandmother. I felt a little lost, suffering severe root rot.

೬ Ho and Paw-Paw had barely driven out of the driveway when the phone rang. I stared at it. Could it be Me-Maw? Would she hang up if I answered? Gingerly I picked up the phone and held it to my ear, not saying anything.

"Hello?" a male voice finally said.

"Hello?" I answered back.

"Kimmey?"

"Will?"

"Hi," he said, "something wrong with the phone?"

"No, I was eating when I picked up the receiver, couldn't get hello out," I said, laughing. I was getting better and better at lies. I'm not sure I liked myself for that. But right that minute I didn't like myself much at all.

"Well," Will said, and I could hear him clearing his throat, "I just wanted to say hi. About Friday night . . ."

"Will, really, I'm sorry—"

"No, Kimmey, it was my fault, I was pushy—"

"No, I was an idiot—"

"No, no, it wasn't your fault," he said, his voice insistent. "It's just that . . . I've never met anyone like you . . ."

I sat down in the chair next to the phone table. Actually, fell down in the chair next to the phone table. "Will—"

"Shh," he said, "let me finish—better yet, let me buy you lunch. Okay?"

"Definitely," I said. "Where and when?"

He laughed. "Noon at the place where we ate Friday night?"

"I'll be there," I said.

"Okay," he said. "Well, 'bye."

" 'Bye," I said and hung up.

That's when I remembered Paw-Paw and Ho had the car.

🐌 "Well, if you're not going to use it . . ." I started.

"Who said I wasn't going to use it?" Pucci insisted, flopping down on the sofa in the tiny bedraggled living area of Ho's Scenic Cruiser.

This was the first time I'd been in Ho's bus. It was even smaller than Paw-Paw's shack, with less furniture, and rusted holes in the walls stuffed with old catalogs. But clean. Everything shone. I pulled up a straight-back chair in front of Pucci. "So what hot plans have you got for the day?" I asked.

"I'm not sure yet. How about if I drive you wherever you need to go."

No way, I thought. "That wouldn't work," I said. "I'm not sure how long I'm going to be."

"I can wait."

The last person in the world I wanted to antagonize right now was Pucci. Which was a feeling I never thought I'd ever feel. Antagonizing Pucci had become almost a life-style for me. But after The Kiss, after the rock-solid support of the night before, how did I tell him I had a lunch date with another man?

"That really won't work," I finally said. I stood up. "I'll see if I can get a taxi to come out here."

Pucci shook his head. "That's silly. When's Paw-Paw expected back?"

"Probably twenty minutes after I need to leave," I said.

"That's okay then," he said, smiling at me. A nice smile. No snideness to it. "You take the rental and if I need to go someplace, I'll borrow Paw-Paw's car."

I bristled. This wasn't right. The whole world had done a flip-flop since the day before. Pucci was being nice, generous, even. And he was calling my grandfather Paw-Paw. How dare he call my grandfather Paw-Paw? How dare he be nice? How dare he lend me his car, putting himself out? I've known the asshole to be sneaky before, but this took the cake!

"Fine!" I said, rather loudly. "I'll take the damn car!"

Pucci raised his left eyebrow, one of the few talents he has besides growing a five-o'clock shadow before noon. The eyebrow came back down and he grinned. "Oh," he said. "I get it. Little slow this morning, Sal. You have a lunch date with your cousin, right, Kruse?"

"Screw you, Pucci," I said. He tossed the keys at me and I caught them in mid-air. I turned and walked out the door.

How dare Pucci screw my life up this way? I thought as I drove rather briskly away from the bridge. How dare he be nice when it's totally out of character? How dare he be generous when generosity is not a moral attribute of someone who has no moral attributes? And above and beyond everything else, how dare he make me feel guilty!!!

Okay, okay, I told myself. Stop thinking about Pucci. The man can drive you nuts. Think about Will. Yes, Will. Beautiful Cousin Will. Who had some definite questions to answer. Like when was the last time *he* saw Armand Dubois? Had he heard from him? What did he know about his father and a member of my family? No, don't ask that, I told myself. You've stirred up enough animosity with that question. Leave it alone. "But what about Barbara Sue?" the nasty little critter with the devil's hat sitting on my left shoulder said. "I mean, okay, so they had a thing in college. But what about now? What is this secret-assignation bit? Huh? And who is the 'she' that needs to keep her mouth shut that Barbara Sue was talking about? And what about their heated words at the cemetery, huh?"

The little critter in the angel's wings sitting on my right shoulder said, "Bug off," and I pulled into the driveway of Tony B's, the restaurant where I planned to meet Will. I went in, finding Will again waiting for me. This time in a suit and tie. He looked so gorgeous I couldn't imagine my hesitation on Friday night or the devil/angel debate in the car. Who wouldn't want to jump this man? No woman I could think of—which is probably exactly what Barbara Sue was thinking. With a man like Jimmy Lynn at home, an ex-beau like Will could look mighty interesting. "Just let her try," said the little angel on the right, with a mighty mean look on her face. I had to agree.

Will stood as I walked to the table, a tentative smile on his face. He took both my hands in his and leaned down, kissing me softly on the mouth. My whole body bristled. *It was better than Pucci's kiss. It had to be. At least as good. Shit. It wasn't. Oh, shit.* I smiled and we both sat down.

"You forgive me for the caveman treatment the other night?" Will asked, stroking my hand.

"If you forgive me for the Pollyanna Purebread crap," I said, stroking back. I wasn't going to think about Will's kiss. No way. It was just that I had too much on my mind right now. It had nothing to do with my attraction to Will or his ability to kiss. Nothing whatsoever.

"How are you doing?" he asked. "How's your grandfather?"

"He's doing better. He's at the doctor's now. We'll find out how much longer he has to stay in the cast."

"Good," Will said, concentrating on my hand.

"Will," I said, "can I ask you a question?"

"You can ask me anything and the answer will probably

be yes," he said, smiling that beautiful dimply smile, the beautiful teeth shining in his alabaster face.

"When was the last time you saw your dad?" I asked. Breaking the spell.

He let go of my hand and leaned back in his chair. "What's this all about?" he asked, frowning, the dimples gone, the teeth hidden, the alabaster skin becoming mottled.

"Will, I know you don't want to hear this, but I'm absolutely positive your mother was mur——"

"You're right. I don't want to hear it. What do you want for lunch?" he said, his total concentration on the blackboard menu on the wall. "The mahimahi looks good. And I can attest to their shrimp salad. It's great."

"Shrimp salad?" The man knew how to divert my attention. "That sounds good. What kind of dressing?"

"Remoulade. Homemade. Really good."

"Ummmm, okay, the shrimp salad and a bowl of gumbo and some of that garlic bread and maybe some rice pudding for dessert?"

He laughed. "Where in the hell are you going to put all that?"

I smiled back. "I have my ways."

The waitress came up (I was thankful it was not the one from Friday night) and took our order, and we sat in a not so companionable silence until Will said, "My office is having a picnic next Saturday. You want to go with me?"

"Sure. Sounds like fun." Root-canal kinda fun. I sighed. "Will, we have to talk about it."

"Kimmey, I don't have to talk about anything I don't want to talk about. That's my privilege as a grown-up."

"Your mother was murdered, Will. And my number-one suspect is your fath——"

"Who in the hell do you think you are?" Will demanded, his face getting red. "Your number-one suspect! Jesus Christ!

Who died and left you in charge? My mother hadn't seen or heard from my father in years! Why would he—" He slumped back in his chair, his hand going to his face and rubbing his eyes. "Kimmey, leave it alone. Let my mother rest in peace. Let my father burn in hell or wherever he is. Just leave it alone."

"Will, I can't—"

"Then figure out if you can eat two lunches," he said, getting up and walking out of the restaurant. The next class, ladies in gentlemen, will be Kimmey Kruse's "How to Win Friends and Influence People."

I'm ashamed to admit I ate both lunches, but stress makes me hungry. I also paid for both lunches, which didn't do my slim-to-nil pocketbook a lot of good. I drove back to the bridge thinking I'd done such a good job of talking to Will, I should have run after him and accused him of sleeping with my cousin Barbara Sue. That would have added insult to injury. Or injury to insult. Whichever. I pulled Pucci's rental into Ho's driveway, getting out and knocking on Ho's pretense of a front door.

"It's open!" came the greeting from inside.

I walked in. To find Pucci with suitcases open on the sofa, Hawaiian shirts folded neatly, socks and underwear piled.

"What are you doing?" I asked, tossing the keys on the couch.

"Packing," he said, his back to me.

"Why?"

"My plane leaves at five o'clock this afternoon."

I went to the sofa and slammed the lid of the suitcase down, barely missing Pucci's fingers. "Why are you leaving?" I demanded.

He looked at me. "Are you willing to talk about what happened between us?"

I threw my arms up in disgust. "What, for God's sake? We kissed! It's not like that was the first time that happened! We kissed in Chicago, too, you know!"

"It wasn't the same thing," he said, his voice quiet.

Well, he was right about that. It wasn't. "Pucci, listen to me. Everyone in my family hates my guts. I just questioned Will about his father, now he hates my guts—"

Pucci perked up. "Yeah?"

I sank down on the couch. "Yeah. He walked out on me without even eating lunch. Left me with the check and everything."

Pucci sat down beside me. "Well, that was certainly rude," he said, taking my hand in his.

I pulled my hand away. "Don't," I said.

He got up and opened the suitcase, throwing in more of his clothing.

"What is this?" I demanded. "Blackmail? If I won't sleep with you you're going to leave me here all alone, right?"

Pucci slammed the lid down. "Wrong!" he said, his voice more heated than I'd ever heard it. "This has nothing to do with sex, Kruse, and you know it! I'm talking about feelings here—"

"Jesus!" I said, moving toward the door. "I don't want to discuss feelings with you, Pucci! I really, really don't!"

"Why? Because you might have to admit you have some for me?"

I walked out Ho's door and headed to Paw-Paw's, going in the back way. If I'd gone by way of the front door I would have seen Me-Maw's car sitting in the driveway and been prepared for her and Aunt Adele sitting with Paw-Paw in the living room. As it was, it came as a bit of a shock.

I DIDN'T REALIZE PUCCI HAD FOLLOWED ME THROUGH THE BACK door until I felt his hands on my arms. It was a good thing they were there. I might have passed out from fright if he hadn't been holding me up.

Paw-Paw sat at the table, his broken leg resting on a chair, a pillow propping it up. Me-Maw and Aunt Adele sat perched on the sofa, their butts barely touching—for fear of contamination, I suppose. All three gray heads turned my way. There was a pregnant pause.

Finally, Paw-Paw said, "Kimberly, you come on in and sit down, *cher.*"

Pucci asked, "Would it be best if I left?"

Aunt Adele and Paw-Paw both looked at Me-Maw. Finally, she said, "No, Mr. Sal. You come sit down, too."

I took the dilapidated easy chair while Pucci picked a straight-back chair, turning it around and sitting astraddle, his arms resting on the back, macho-style. I found it strangely attractive, even as terrified as I was. Go figure.

Me-Maw straightened her shoulders, gripping her purse tightly in both hands, and said, "Kimberly Anne. What we gonna tell you ain't nobody around here know 'cept me and you aunt Adele and you aunt Laurina and you paw-paw. You gotta swear on all that you hold holy that it won't go no further." She looked at Pucci. "You too, Mr. Sal."

Pucci held up his right hand. "I swear on my mother's eyes," he said.

I held up my right hand. "Me, too," I said, though I wasn't sure if I was swearing on *my* mother's eyes or *Pucci's* mother's eyes. I would prefer God thought I was talking about Pucci's mom.

Me-Maw sighed. Then she began to talk. "Our daddy he die when I was twelve. He weren't no more than thirty year old, neither. Died in a accident at the mill where he worked. Cut off his arm and bled to death 'fore they could get him to a hospiddle. We had a little piece a land outside a Armentine, fifty, sixty acre. Mama she try to work the land her own self, with me and my sisters helping her, but without no money coming in, we lost the place to back taxes less than a year after Daddy die."

Me-Maw looked at Aunt Adele, who nodded encouragement.

"Anyway," Me-Maw said, "we hadda move so we went into town, into Armentine, and got us a room back of an old aunt's place. Room littler than this room," she said, indicating the living room of Paw-Paw's shack. "Mama and us five girls. Mama took in washing and I quit school and went to work at the dairy, milking cows. I was big and strong and they thought I was older than twelve, but I weren't. I was the oldest; me, then Adele, then Laurina, then Blanche, then Clothilde.

"We didn't have a lotta money. We wasn't even what they call dirt-poor, 'cause we done lost that. All we had was that little room, and that mean old aunt thought we should do all her housework and her cooking for her since we in that little room. And we did. When I was fourteen and Adele was—what, Adele?" Me-Maw asked.

"Always been one year younger than you, Genevieve. I be thirteen when it happened."

"That's right. Anyway, little Clothilde, the baby, she be only seven year old. Come the influenza and it took her bad. She die a month later. I thought it was gonna kill Mama out-right. She never was much the same after that. You lose a baby, you don't get over that."

We all sat silently, thinking about that loss. Then Me-Maw said, "We just go on like that for a long time. Then I meet you paw-paw when I was nineteen and we get married. You aunt Adele and you uncle Lester they betrothed. It was 1934. In the middle of the Great Depression. But you paw-paw and you uncle Lester, they both had jobs, and they promise they gonna help out Mama, or me and Adele, we don' marry 'em, yeah, Adele?"

Adele smiled at her big sister. "That right, Genevieve. Family come first."

Me-Maw heaved a big sigh. "Blanche, she be fifteen year old that year, 1934."

Adele took Me-Maw's hand and they sat silently looking at each other. Finally, Me-Maw squeezed Adele's hand, patted it and said, "that when Armand DuBois see Blanche for the first time."

Adele said, "Blanche, she be the pretty one. Me and you me-maw, even you aunt Laurina, we nothing to brag about, but Blanche, she *jolle blanc*. Pretty little blonde. And sweet. Had the sweetest disposition of any of Mama's babies, ain't that right, Genevieve?"

"That true." Me-Maw looked off into space. "I betcha nowdays, in the schools, they call Blanche slow. We just call her Blanche." Another huge sigh lifted Me-Maw's bosom, then slowly dropped it back in place.

"Armand DuBois come from Lafayette down to Armentine to move in with his me-maw. We don't know nothing 'bout him 'cept he so *jolle*. He be my age but he come courtin' Blanche. In them days, girls marry young, so we don't think nothing 'bout it. Me and Tobert we chaperone them, go where they go. We had some times, yeah, Tobert?"

Paw-Paw smiled at Me-Maw. "Yeah, Genevieve, we had us some times."

"That Armand he so sweet to Blanche. Buy her flowers and candy. Take her nice places. We don't know where he get his money, we ask and he say, 'Oh, a little a this, a little a that," Aunt Adele said.

"Then Blanche she get sick," Me-Maw said. "Adele still at home and she come get me and we take Blanche to my place, a little room me and Tobert had behind his daddy's store. I was already with you aunt Lucielle, though I wasn't showing much yet, but I been through the morning sickness and I knowed what was wrong with Blanche. I say to her, 'Girl, who done this to you?' And she cry. She knowed she done wrong. And she say, a course, that it was Armand DuBois."

Paw-Paw held up his hand. "Genevieve say to me, 'You go get that Armand and you tell him they gotta get married quick.' I say you bet and I go where his me-maw stay but she say Armand don' live there no more. She say, maybe he over at the Dew Drop Inn where he like to go. So I go over there and, sure 'nuff, there he be, sitting there with this tarted-up ole gal. I say, 'Armand, I gotta talk with you,' and he say okay and we go outside and I tell him Blanche with child and why for he go and do that to a sweet girl like Blanche. He say he love her and he gonna marry her. Say he couldn't help hisself, she so *jolle blanc*. So I say, 'Okay, you come on over to my place this evening and we work out when you two tie the knot,' and he say okay."

Me-Maw sighed. "Don't guess I gotta tell you Armand DuBois he never show up. Hightailed it back to Lafayette. When Mama find out about Blanche she get sick, and the bigger Blanche got, the sicker Mama got. We had to try to keep Blanche hid, but it's kinda hard in a little room like that. That mean old aunt found out and started spreading the word round the whole town. Made Mama and the girls move out of that room. The room me and Tobert had was even littlier than Mama's room, but we took 'em in 'cause they had noplace else to go. Adele she go ahead and marry you uncle Lester and they staying at Lester's mama's house with all his brothers and sisters, and they be a ton of 'em, but Adele be one less mouth we gotta feed. And you aunt Lucielle, she already come, so I got me a houseful with my new baby and Mama and Laurina and Blanche big as a house."

Aunt Adele took Me-Maw's hand again. Me-Maw's voice was soft, in a far-off place. "Blanche's baby come too soon. We call the midwife and she come but the baby breech. By the time she get it out the baby dead. Blanche die an hour later. Bled to death, and weren't nothing we could do 'cept watch."

"Mama die two month later," Adele said. "She jest didn't wanna live no more, I guess."

"That no-good Armand he come back after Blanche gone," Paw-Paw said, "and me and you uncle Lester we go find him. We gonna kill the sumgun. But he knowed we was comin' and he had the Gunfey boys with him, all of 'em bigger than houses. They beat the shit—'cuse me, ladies—they beat the crap outta me and Lester. Then Armand say how he be with all them Foret girls, calls 'em white trash, says mean, terrible things about Blanche."

"That when Tobert and Lester decide to move us to Port Arthur. Refineries hiring then, even if it were the Depression, and we took Laurina and Lucielle and we moved. Never heard nothing more about Armand DuBois till my aunt write and say Leticia she gonna marry him. Me and Leticia we been writing letters ever month to each other since I left Armentine. But she never say a word in her letters 'bout Armand DuBois." Me-Maw shook her head. "I call Leticia up long distance. I say, 'Why for you gonna marry that no-good white trash?' And she say, 'Genevieve, he love me, he wanna marry me.' " Me-Maw shook her head. "Leticia she so old by then, been takin' care her sick mama most her life, she don' know nothin' 'cept this *jolle* man he ask her to marry. I tell her, 'Leticia, you marry that trash I never had me no cousin named Leticia. You hear?' "

Me-Maw shook her head. "Guess she don' hear," she said quietly.

I got up from my chair and walked up between Me-Maw and Aunt Adele and put my arms around them both, kissing first my grandmother on the cheek, and then my aunt. I squatted down in front of them.

"It the family shame, Kimberly Anne. Now you gotta keep the secret," Me-Maw said.

I took the old, work-scarred hand in mine. "Me-Maw," I said, "it wasn't Blanche's fault. A man like Armand—there was no way he wouldn't have gotten what he wanted from her."

Me-Maw shook her head. "I know what Oprah say and Montel and Donahue. Victims." She shook her head again. "Different times, different ways, *cher*. Different ways."

I fixed us all iced tea, after Me-Maw watched me wash the glasses and pour boiling water over them, and we all sat down. "Mrs. Broussard," Pucci said, "I'm so sorry for your losses."

"That were a long time ago," Me-Maw said.

"Yes, ma'am," Pucci said, "and sometimes the pain can turn with time from sour to sweet, but it's still pain."

If my grandparents hadn't been in the room right then, I might have jumped him. I have this thing about poetic sensitivity.

Me-Maw smiled at Pucci. "You a good boy, Mr. Sal," she said. "You mama—she alive?"

"Yes, ma'am."

"You good to you mama?"

Pucci smiled. "I have Sunday dinner with her every week, talk to her on the phone every Wednesday. I'm sending her and my aunt on a trip to Florida this winter."

Me-Maw sighed. "Sometimes I wished we had us a boy, Tobert," she said.

I made a mental note to remind my mother to call a little more often.

"So," I said, "you never saw Cousin Leticia again?"

"Not till the day she die," Me-Maw said. She looked at me. "You think Armand done that, yeah, girl?"

I nodded. "He certainly has a history of abuse. I'm not sure why he'd do it now, but if he thought he could get something out of her—"

"Armand he always figure a way to get something outta a woman," Paw-Paw said.

I sat back in my chair, thinking. "Did Leticia actually ever divorce Armand?"

"Oo-eee, girl," Me-Maw said, "they ain't never been no divorce in this family till you up and done it." She gave me her stern look.

I smiled sweetly. "Different times, Me-Maw, different ways," I said. "So they were still legally married. Under Louisiana law, if a person dies intestate, does the spouse naturally inherit?" I asked.

"Say what?" Me-Maw said.

"If Cousin Leticia didn't have a will, then, normally, her estate would go to her husband."

"She don' have no estate," Aunt Adele said, "just a little old house in Armentine."

"That's what Kimmey's trying to say, Mrs. Romero," Pucci said. "Her house, any money in the bank, her furniture, everything she owned would go to her husband if she didn't leave a will specifying that her belongings were to go to her son or someone else."

Everyone looked at Me-Maw. She looked back. Finally, she said, "Well, I don't know if she had a will. Best talk to Willard about that."

Right, I thought. He'd really welcome that question from me.

Thinking out loud, I said, "I can't seem to trace Armand past twenty years ago. Except for Will. He says he remembers seeing his dad like ten or fifteen years ago, but Enic said he hadn't seen or heard from him in close to thirty, and Dorisca Judice"—the mention of that name made everyone shudder, especially Pucci—"says she hasn't seen him in over twenty years—"

"Oooo, that lying such-and-such," Aunt Adele said. "Genevieve, you remember that big storm back in seventy-eight when we hadda go over to the church to help with evacuees coming from the coast?"

Me-Maw nodded. "Sure do. Never dished up so much gumbo in my whole life, yeah?"

"Well, I was driving to the church when I seen Dorisca in that red hussy car of hers and she had Armand with her. Liked to bust a gut when I seen 'em, too. I say something to one of the ladies at the church and she say she hear Dorisca had a man living with her. A real good-lookin' man. I say I know who that man is and Dorisca Judice she can have him."

"In 1978?" I said, counting on my fingers. I've never been very good at math.

"Fifteen years ago," Pucci said. "And Dorisca definitely said twenty. She said she hadn't seen Armand since she moved to Port Arthur."

I grinned at him. "So you were actually able to listen?"

"Shut up, Kruse."

"Well, she lying," Aunt Adele said. " 'Cause I seen 'em. Big as day."

⟨⟩ That night I had What a Hoot. Pucci drove me over there and we discussed our plans in the car. I was rapidly running out of clothes—I'm not big on handwashing, and Paw-Paw doesn't have a washer and dryer—so I borrowed a little of this and a little of that until I was a thing of beauty. A Hawaiian shirt from Pucci worn over the top of my Bill Blass long johns (okay, so I wash those—like every night!) and a pair of pillow-ticking overalls from Paw-Paw, worn with my hot-pink high-tops. The hot-pink baseball cap over my fright-wig hair and I was ready to go.

"First thing in the morning, we go by Dorisca's," Pucci said. "I'll stay in the car—"

"Coward—"

"And you go in and give her some shit. Tell her we know she was seen with Armand right here in Port Arthur—"

"I know what to say!"

"—no more than fifteen years ago, so we know she's lying. Get mean with her. That kind should crumple pretty quick . . ."

I grinned. "She'd crumple quicker if you went in by yourself. Laid on a little charm—"

"You're a sick woman, Kruse." He grinned. "Generally, I like that in my women."

We pulled up in front of What a Hoot. "What are you going to do for four hours?" I asked him, getting out of the car. I noticed he turned the engine off and was getting out, too.

"Thought I'd catch your gig," he said.

"Not without paying," I retorted.

Well, it wasn't going to be so bad. There were thirty-seven people in the Tuesday-evening class. There would also be that many in the Thursday-night class, because Tuesday was just the first half of their eight-hour penance. Thirty-seven people times $3.50 came to $129.50. Multiply that by two and it was a whopping $259. (Okay, so I had to use a calculator, but I figured it out on my own.) If Saturday's class was at least as many as the previous Saturday's, I might be able to have an actual income.

Pucci, of course, was the biggest heckler in the room. But I was used to his trash and most of our shtick actually went over fairly well. In another life we might make a good team. But not in this one, thank you very much.

When we pulled into Paw-Paw's driveway, Pucci looked off to the left, to what used to be swampland the last time I'd visited Paw-Paw under the bridge. But the restaurant at the front of the marina had built an extension—a bar and grill—on landfill at the dead end of the marina road.

"What's that?" Pucci asked, pointing to the lights of Dominque's (pronounced "Domain's") on the Neches.

"It's a restaurant, part of the one up there," I said, pointing toward the entrance to the marina.

"They serve booze?" he asked.

"Does the Pope poop in the woods?"

"Wanna drink?"

I got out of the car. "Yeah. Let's get Paw-Paw and Ho and go check it out," I said, heading for the door of the shack.

Paw-Paw and Ho were in the living room playing forty-two, which is a domino game I have never figured out how to play.

"You Me-Maw called," Paw-Paw said when we walked in. "She talk to Willard on the telephone and he say his mama don' have no will. So maybe you right, girl."

I nodded, not wanting to talk about Will or his mama at the moment. "Y'all wanna go over to Dominque's for a beer?" I asked.

Ho nodded and Paw-Paw said, "Well, girl, I give up spirits thirty-five year ago, but I have me a soda pop and watch y'all, yeah?"

We gathered up Paw-Paw and his crutches and walked the fifty-some-odd yards to Dominque's on the crushed-oystershell road.

Dominque's was two rooms—a small bar and a large dining area. Not a soul was in either place. All the action seemed to be outside on the deck that ran the full width of the bar and grill, jutting out into the waters of the Neches River.

A woman, heavyset and matronly, with brassy-blond hair and an easy disposition, popped out of a door in the wall and asked, "Y'all wanna stay in here or outside?"

"Is there room outside?" Pucci asked.

She grinned, exposing tobbaco-stained teeth rimmed with decay. "Always make room. Come on."

We went out onto the deck, where patrons helped move tables and chairs to fit us in. The woman took our drink order and disappeared through the glass doors into the dining room.

We found ourselves squeezed in between two tables of about five men each, with one lonely woman at each table.

Paw-Paw nodded to one of the men and said, "Bernard, how you be?"

"Tobert," Bernard, a man younger than Paw-Paw but a great deal older than the other men at the table, said. *"Il n'a in bon boute."*

"Comment ca va?" Paw-Paw asked.

The man held his hand out straight and wiggled it, the Cajun non-verbal *"comme se comme sa."*

"How the shrimping?" Paw-Paw asked.

"She-it," Bernard said. "Ain't no shrimp left in dese waters, man, I tell you what. Done been shrimped to death, I tellin' you."

The waitress came out with our drinks and we sipped. I looked guardedly at Ho, who was quietly drinking the wine he'd ordered and ignoring the conversation. I worried about the possibility of a scene because Ho was with us. Only a few years before, the waters around Port Arthur had erupted when the KKK came to town to avenge the white shrimpers who were accusing the newly arrived Vietnamese shrimpers of illegal fishing practices.

But the man, Bernard, turned to Ho and said, "You boy having any luck up around Sabine?"

Ho said something in garbled Vietnamese and French and Bernard, who, like Paw-Paw, seemed to have no trouble understanding, said, "She-it, dat what I thought. Ain't no shrimp nowhere no way, I tell you what!"

In a lull in the conversation I told Pucci, "Did you know that Paw-Paw can taste a shrimp and tell you whether it was caught in the lake or in the Gulf?"

Pucci raised his one eyebrow at Paw-Paw. "Oh, really?"

Paw-Paw grinned. "Oh, hell, Bo, I can look at 'em, smell 'em, I know the difference."

Bernard laughed. "Like that some big deal. My grandbaby can do that and she's a girl!"

I kept my mouth shut. It was an effort, but when in Rome . . .

"You hear about that depression out in the Gulf?" Paw-Paw asked Bernard.

"Hell, ain't no depression no more—upgraded to a tropical storm. Call it George, ha! You believe that?"

"That why you in for the night?"

"She-it, I be in for a couple day, I reckon, ole George keeps upgrading."

"What the radio say?"

"Say look good for a hurrkin."

A homemade shrimp boat was pulled up to the side of Dominque's deck. Pucci nodded his head toward it and asked Bernard, "That yours?"

Bernard nodded. "Sure is."

"How often do you go out?"

Bernard spit a wad of chewing tobacco into a cup on the table. "Ever day. That's a forty-footer. Used to go out on three-, four-day trips. Back when there was enough shrimp make it worthwhile, yeah?" He spit again. "She-it, them was the days."

"But you go out every day now?"

"Yeah, pull a single rig net off the back. Some days come back with a shit pot—some days I come back with my dick in my hand—'scuse me, little lady," he said to me.

I nodded.

"Count's been down ever year," Bernard said. "Nowdays we lucky if we get a hunnard and fifty, two hunnard pounds a day."

Considering shrimp was going from anywhere between six dollars and twelve dollars a pound in Austin, I said, "Sounds like a lot to me."

"No way to make a living, little lady," Bernard said.

"What did it used to be like?" I asked.

" 'Bout double that."

I glanced over at the boat. "When you went out on three-day trips, where'd you sleep?"

Bernard held out his hand. "Come on, ti-cher, I show you. Bo," he said, nodding his head at Pucci, "you wanna see a real-live shrimp boat, you being a Yankee and all?"

Pucci stood up. "How'd you know I was a Yankee?" he asked as we walked toward the shrimper.

Bernard laughed. "You opened you mouth, didn't you?"

The boat was small, when you thought about spending three days on it in the open sea. Forty feet, it was painted white with bright blue on the rails and the cabin. The cabin was a square room with a large windshield in front, with the wheel and gears above the windshield. Two bunks on the wall opposite the wheel were bare now of mattresses and appeared to be used for spreading out maps and lunch (by the used KFC bucket sitting there). Above the wheel, as Bernard pointed out, were the radar, VHF radio and CB radio, and the depth finder.

I told Bernard how much shrimp were going for in Austin. His eyes lit up. He walked to the rail of the shrimper and leaned over toward Dominque's deck. "Antone!" he called to one of the men sitting at the table where he'd been. "You still got that panel truck you brother sold you?"

"Yeah, I got it."

"Good, boy, 'cause dis weekend, we going to Austin sell us some shrimp!"

As we were turning to leave, I saw a woman walking up the ramp on the side of Dominque's toward land. The woman, from the back, had bleached-blond hair and clothing that could only belong to Dorisca Judice. There was a man with her—tall, slender, with graying hair . . .

I grabbed Pucci's arm. "It's him!"

"What? Who?"

I pointed at the retreating figures as I hurriedly got off the shrimper, jumping to the deck of Dominque's and hurrying toward the little gate that led to the ramp. The gate was locked.

"It's Armand DuBois! It's gotta be!" I yelled.

Pucci grabbed the gate but it remained locked. I ran to the glass doors into the dining room of Dominque's and hurriedly through that to the front door, Pucci hot on my trail. By the time we got to the crushed-oystershell road in front of the restaurant, the pair was nowhere to be seen.

It was cloudy and muggy when we set out for Dorisca's Wednesday morning. The overcast sky, however, didn't seem to deter the heat any. There wasn't a breath of wind and the humidity seemed to settle around us, thick and wet like a good gumbo.

"Told you that shit about Blanche's husband being eaten by an alligator was stupid," Pucci said.

"Well, it may have been stupid but it was family folklore. Wish it was true. That he had been eaten by an alligator. Armand, I mean."

"Wouldn't that have been nice?" Pucci turned the air-conditioning up a notch.

"Do you realize that if my aunt Blanche had actually married Armand, she would have been Blanche DuBois?" I asked.

"That's true," Pucci said, looking at me with his brows knit.

"Like in, 'I depend upon the kindness of strangers'?" I quoted, giving it my worst Deep South accent.

"Oh," Pucci said. Then tried his own quote, yelling, " 'Stella!' " at the top of his lungs. Marlon Brando he wasn't.

We drove silently for a moment, then he said, "Are we ever going to talk about us?"

"I take it you didn't catch that flight yesterday evening."

"Yeah, Kruse, I'm in Chicago now. It's a lot cooler there. I'm thinking of going to a Cubs day game today."

"Sarcasm has never become you, Pucci."

"Then don't give me so many damn reasons to use it." He sighed. "You're right, Kruse. I'm still here." He looked at me. "Doesn't that mean something to you?"

I looked out the window, wishing there were something out there to distract my attention. Unfortunately there wasn't. "I'm glad you stayed," I finally said, my voice smaller than I'd have preferred.

"Are you?"

I sighed. "What do you want from me, Pucci?" I said, finally looking at him.

"Declarations of undying love would be nice," he said.

I snorted. "Yeah? And what would you do with them?" I asked.

He looked at me. "Love you back," he said.

Oh, boy, I thought. I was saved from a response by our turn onto Newhope Street.

We pulled into Dorisca's driveway, parking behind the cherry-red Mustang, the white convertible top up, its black plastic window clouded with age. As we walked up to the driveway, we could see Dorisca in the driver's seat. She was staring off into space. "Dorisca," I said, putting my hand on her shoulder.

It was at this point I noticed the plastic flamingo sitting upside down in the back seat, the steel rod used to ram the flamingo into the ground instead rammed into the back of Dorisca Judice's head, holding her upright in the seat and turning the nasty bleached-blond beehive even nastier with bits of dried earth, grass, and blood.

I lost my breakfast. Which seemed to be as sensible an action at the time as anything else I could think of.

Chapter

12

"I TOLD THAT BOZO EARLIER ALL ABOUT LETICIA DUBOIS," I SAID, my face tight and my arms crossed over my chest.

"Uh-huh. An' what bozo would that be, ma'am?" Buddy Don Keehoe asked.

"Sergeant Lloyd, Detective Keehoe," Pucci said. "Ms. Kruse reported what she suspected as a homicide to Sergeant Lloyd last week. We believe there may be a connection between Mrs. DuBois's death and Mrs. Judice's death."

" 'We *believe* there *may* be?' " I mimicked. "You're damned straight there's a connection! Two women have been murdered, and I'm pretty damned sure the murderer is a man by the name of Armand DuBois."

"Uh-huh," Buddy Don said, leaning against his unmarked squad car and playing with a toothpick stuck in the corner of his mouth. He wore a burnt-orange leisure suit over a brown-and-white western-style shirt. His wide green-and-brown-striped tie clashed miserably with the unborn-calf-skin boots. Buddy Don Keehoe was a fashion statement. I just didn't want to hear what he had to say. "And what makes you think that, ma'am?" he asked.

I know when I'm being condescended to. I've always had a great grasp on male porker syndrome. And this guy, to borrow from Paw-Paw, was et up with it.

I very painstakingly went over all the facts in the case against Armand DuBois and the finding of Dorisca Judice's body.

Buddy Don said, "Uh-huh. And where might this Armand DuBois be?"

"At this point in time, I'm not actually aware of his location," I said.

"Uh-huh," Buddy Don said, "and when was the last time you was aware of his location, ma'am?" He was one of those men born with hair so white they usually had the nickname Cotton. His ruddy complexion was so ruddy it was actually a bright red.

I looked at Pucci. He shrugged and leaned against the unmarked squad car, unconsciously, or very consciously, siding with the enemy—that is, Buddy Don Keehoe.

"I know he was seen here in Port Arthur in 1978," I said. "And I think we saw him last night—I'm sure we did—"

Pucci interrupted. "We have no idea if that was him last night, Kruse. We're not even sure if it was Dorisca—"

"I'm sure—"

"Uh-huh. In 1978, you say?" Buddy Don said. "Well, now, that does narrow it down a bit, don't it?" The asshole grinned at me.

I had this overwhelming urge to grab him by the scruff of his neck and throw him up against his own car, but as he was well over six feet, I doubted I could reach the scruff of his neck. Even if I could identify what a scruff might actually be.

I instead walked to Pucci's rental. "I'll wait in the car," I told Pucci over my shoulder.

"Good idea," he said.

"Uh-huh," Buddy Don said.

☙ "Dorisca Judice is dead," I said into the phone.

"I'm so sorry," Phoebe said. "Is she another relative?"

"No, Phoebe. She's the woman I told you about that ran off with Will's father that time. The one who was coming on to Pucci so horribly?"

Phoebe snickered. "Oh. Her. Well, you said she was getting up in years, which was part of the fun with Pucci, right?"

"Yeah, but she didn't die from natural causes," I said.

Phoebe sighed. "What are you getting yourself into this time, Kimberly?"

"I've told you from the beginning that Cousin Leticia was murdered."

"Right. The two-wasp theory."

"You never believed me!" I accused her. "You're as bad as everyone else." I fumed for half a minute. "Well, now do you believe me?"

"Because Dorisca Judice was murdered?" Phoebe asked.

"Yes!"

"Well, Kimmey, the way Dorisca got around, she could have been killed by a jealous wife or a vengeful lover, or, with the description of her yard that you gave me, her neighbors!"

"You know, it used to be fun talking to you on the phone. But it isn't anymore."

"Would you prefer I tell you only what you want to hear?" Phoebe asked.

"Yes!" I answered and hung up.

I heard the sound of a car pulling into the driveway and

went to the front window to look out. It was a Port Arthur squad car, bringing Pucci back. He and ole Buddy Don seemed to hit it off just great after I'd gone to Pucci's car, and a few minutes after I got in and rolled the window down for air, Pucci had come over and given me the keys, advising me that I go on back to the marina and wait for him. I burned rubber getting off Newhope Street and didn't even get a ticket. 'Course, I'd like to see 'em try!

Pucci got out of the car, leaning in the open window and laughing at something the cop inside said. He looked at me at the window, leaned back inside the car and both laughed again.

I went to the front door and locked it.

Pucci came in anyway. The lock didn't work well, since the doorjamb and the door hardly met.

Paw-Paw was in the bedroom taking a nap, so I couldn't escape in there. I headed instead to the bathroom, the only other room in the shack that had a door.

By the nearness of Pucci's voice I knew he was leaning against the door. By the tone I knew he was as big an asshole as I'd always thought him to be. "Hey, Kruse," he said, smirking (I may not have been able to see it but I can tell a smirk when I hear it, by God), "you want to come out of there and discuss what the police have to say?"

I didn't answer.

"Or are you going to act like the spoiled brat you are and stay hidden in the ladies' room all day?"

I didn't answer.

His voice was farther away when he said, "I think I'll heat up some of this gumbo your me-maw brought over yesterday." A small silence. "Ummm. This smells good. Lookee here, shrimp and crawfish. And what's this? Crab? Your me-maw puts crab in her gumbo? I think I'll just stick this in the microwave. Hit one minute. You think one minute'll be enough or should I hit two? Yeah, you're right. Two. We want it good and steamy."

I could hear the whir of the microwave. Then the smell began to seep my way. That gumbo smell that smells like nothing else in this world. And, on top of that, it was my me-maw's gumbo smell.

The timer went off. I could hear Pucci opening the door of the microwave. "Umm-umm," he said. "Sure does smell good! Do we have any of that French bread left over from the other night? Boy, that would be good. Dip that hard French bread in the gumbo! Umm-umm. Ah, here it is. There's plenty left. I'll just get me a spoon—"

I opened the bathroom door. "You're an asshole," I said, taking one of the two spoons in his hand and sitting down at the table to the bowl of gumbo and plate of bread he'd already prepared for me. Umm, it was good. And the hard French bread dunked in the gumbo—ambrosia!

I got up from the table. "I think there's some *boudin* in the fridge," I said. "Go great with this."

I pulled out a link of *boudin,* stuck it in the microwave for a minute, cut it in two and gave half to Pucci.

"What is this?" he asked, looking at the rice and other ingredients inside the sausage skin.

"*Boudin,*" I said. "It's great. Eat it."

I scooped some out of the skin and smeared it on a piece of French bread, popping it into my mouth. Pucci followed.

"Umm," he said. "Good."

"It's blood sausage," I said, smirking.

He grinned back. "Honey, I'm Italian. That doesn't gross me out."

"Asshole," I said.

Having a keen awareness of my own psyche, the word "petulant" began gnawing at my brain. I threw it bones, such as, "He's an asshole," and "He delights in pushing my buttons," but the word just grew and grew, threatening to modify my behavior.

I figured if my mouth had to be open, the best way to deal with it was by stuffing it with food. Which I did judiciously.

"Well, she weren't the nicest woman in the world," Paw-Paw said, "but you get to be our age you shouldn't have ta go that way. No, sir, ain't fair."

"You're right, Tobert," Pucci said, "it's not fair. Murder never is."

"What did that stupid Buddy Don have to say?" I asked.

Pucci glanced over at me and raised an eyebrow. "Now you're interested?"

I studied my fingernails. "It was just a question."

"He's going to put the paperwork in to exhume Leticia's body. There wasn't an autopsy—"

"I told them before the funeral—"

He just looked at me. I shut up. "There wasn't an autopsy, so now, with this possible connection to Dorisca's murder, he thinks they might have reasonable cause to exhume the body."

"Will's not going to like that," I said.

"Can hardly blame him," Pucci said.

"Meanwhile?" I asked, wishing I could raise an eyebrow, one of the few talents I don't possess.

"Meanwhile, there will be a routine investigation into Dorisca's murder. One of her neighbors got up to go fishing around five o'clock this morning and saw Dorisca sitting in the Mustang and thought it was a little strange, but he just said good morning and went on."

"Did she respond?" I asked.

"He couldn't remember."

"Why would she be sitting in the car at five in the morning?" I demanded.

"She probably wouldn't have been. She didn't seem the early-riser type," Pucci said. "Unless she was just getting home. But I'd venture to guess that she was dead at five and had been sitting in the car since the night before."

"When will we find out?" I asked.

"The medical examiner's autopsying her now. Pinpointing time of death is not as easy as TV would have you believe. We can probably narrow it down within a few hours, but that's as good as it usually gets, unless you have an eyewitness to the killing who's wearing an accurate watch and happens to look at it at precisely the right time."

"Who'd wanna go and kill that silly ole woman?" Paw-Paw asked, shaking his head.

"Armand DuBois," I said. "She's probably been seeing him off and on for the past twenty years and told him we were looking for him. He got scared that she'd tell us where he is and he offed her. End of story."

"End of scenario," Pucci said. "There are other explanations."

"Like what?" I demanded.

"A jealous wife, a jealous lover. The taste police." He grinned. "Oh, and that guy we saw her with last night is a retired Port Arthur policeman. Very married. But it certainly wasn't Armand DuBois."

All I wanted to do was go in the bathroom and shut the door.

❧ The phone rang. I went over and picked it up, hearing a voice say, "What have you done, Kimmey? What the hell have you done?"

"Will?"

"Who in the hell do you think you are—"

"Will! Wait! What's wrong?"

"They're talking about exhuming my mother's body!"

"Will, it wasn't my idea! But Dorisca Judice has been murdered—"

"Who?"

"Dorisca Judice. Remember, she was the woman at the reunion in the ugly yellow—"

"What in the hell has that got to do with exhuming my mother?"

"She was your father's lover, Will." There was a silence. "We think your father killed her, too, Will—"

"You are out of your mind," Will said, his diction precise and eloquent, though the words were neither. "I cannot believe you will not allow my mother to rest in peace. What have I ever done to you, Kimmey, except try to love you? Can you answer me that? Why are you trying to make a bad thing worse?"

"I'm not doing this, Will, honest," I said, trying to find someone else to blame it all on. "The police think there's a connection—"

"Why would they? If you hadn't told them what you did about my mother?"

Well, I couldn't answer that one.

"Will—"

"Stay out of my life, Kimmey. Stay the fuck out of my life!"

The line went dead in my hand.

❧ The police called Pucci and me down to the station late that afternoon to sign our statements. The Port Arthur Police Station was downtown, a place I hadn't been to in years. Since all my relatives lived in the outlying areas, there was very little reason to go there. But I remembered Paw-Paw once taking me downtown when I was little to buy me a birthday present at J. C. Penney's—a pink woolly sweater. Then we'd gone down the street to Kress's five-and-dime for matching pink hair bows and my first real nail polish—Pretty As a Picture Pink. And then we'd gone next door to Walgreen's for strawberry ice-cream sodas at their fountain.

For years after that, whenever I thought of Port Arthur, my thoughts were clouded in a fuzzy pink aura, and my tenth birthday has always stood out in my mind as one of my best. That day on the way to the car we'd walked by the Sabine Hotel, big and majestic, where oilmen were talking business on the sidewalk, smoking cigars and discussing the price per barrel. Paw-Paw had tipped his hat to a man who stood there, a big man in a fancy suit, who'd held out his hand and said, "Broussard," and shook my Paw-Paw's hand. That was the day I knew my paw-paw was an important man.

I drove the car down Proctor Street, the heart of Port Arthur. We passed something new that hadn't been there when I was little—a park with a huge statue of the Queen of Vietnam (an almond-eyed Virgin Mary) across the street from the Parish Peace Vietnamese Catholic Church. Farther down Proctor was what had been the Proctor Street Baptist Church. It was now the Hua Buumon Buddhist Temple, complete with new face and roof. The faces on the street were black or Asian. White flight had hit Port Arthur with a vengeance.

We passed J. C. Penney's and Kress's and Walgreen's and the Hotel Sabine—all boarded up and waiting for the demolition crew. We turned off Proctor heading for the seawall that separated Port Arthur from the Inter-Coastal Canal. The police station was across the street from the seawall.

Trying to get the image of the ghost of downtown Port

Arthur out of my mind, I asked Pucci, "You think we can get that picture of Armand DuBois Dorisca had hanging on her wall and have it computer-enhanced to age him? Get an idea of who we're looking for."

He shrugged. "I don't know if the Port Arthur PD has the facilities for that," he said. "Might have to send it to Houston. Take a while."

"Okay, where do we go from here?" I asked.

Pucci looked at me, the eyebrow raised. "We? This is now official police business. Buddy Don's been courteous to me because I'm a brother officer, even if I am a Yankee. But I don't think he's going to appreciate much interference on my part, much less yours."

I sat back and thought nasty things about Buddy Don, Pucci, and every man I'd ever met. We drove on in silence.

The week dragged by. My What a Hoot Thursday night was a whopping success. They loved me. Of course, what's not to love? I was funny, charming, adorable, and perky. Who could ask for more while doing penance? I even had one guy ask me for a date. He wasn't my type, but it was the thought that counts.

Friday Phoebe finally faxed me my defensive-driving file from my cabinet at home and I worked on it, incorporating the new material I'd worked up since I'd begun at What a Hoot. I called my agent and had to tell her twice who I was before she remembered. Not a good sign. I called a couple of club owners in different parts of the country, reminding them how funny I was and how they'd probably love to have me on their stage yet again. One did, one didn't. I set a tentative gig for the fall at a club in Altoona, Pensylvania.

A few important things happened in the latter part of that week: Erica's daughter Bianca ran away on "All My Children," a woman from Albany, New York, became a five-time champion on "Jeopardy!" and they replayed my favorite "Mary Tyler Moore Show," the one where Chuckles the Clown, while dressed as a peanut in a parade, is shucked to death by an elephant.

The comedian who worked with me on Saturdays (okay, the young man desperately trying to become a comedian) asked me to switch times with him, so I lazed around most of Saturday morning and went into What a Hoot around noon to start the 1-P.M.-to-5-P.M. shift.

I saw little of Pucci during that time. I had no idea what he was doing, but saw the rental leave and return at strange hours. I didn't ask. Paw-Paw and Ho tried to teach me to play forty-two, but I only succeeded in dropping the entire set of dominoes on the floor and spent almost an hour trying to find where the last one had escaped to. It had somehow lodged itself between the cushions of the couch. (You play forty-two with a box of twenty-eight double six dominoes. It is my theory that when I spilled the dominoes, there had only been twenty-seven and the entire incident was a ruse cooked up by Paw-Paw and Ho to find that elusive twenty-eighth domino. Men are like that. Sneaky bastards, and they only get sneakier the older they get.)

Me-Maw called, demanding my presence in church on Sunday morning. I went to her house and picked her up.

Driving to Aunt Adele's house to get her, Me-Maw said, "Willard he called me, yeah?"

"He did?" I asked, almost swerving off the road.

"He be real mad at you, *cher,*" she said.

"That I am keenly aware of, Me-Maw. He cussed me out on the phone."

Me-Maw went "tsk, tsk." "He had no call to do that, *cher.* You jest trying to help."

"That's what I told him," I said, or whined, or whatever.

"He say they dig up his mama's body on Friday," Me-Maw said.

"Really? They exhumed her already?"

"That what he say. He say he don' make 'em get no court order 'cause they jest do it anyway, yeah? So he give his permission to go ahead and dig her on up."

I nodded my head. The wisest decision on his part. He could have made them wait for the court order, but what would have been the point?

I hadn't prayed in a long time, probably not since my churchgoing days of junior high. My parents, the liberals, gave me permission at the age of thirteen to make my own decision on whether or not I wanted to attend church. I, of course, opted for sleeping in of a Sunday morning.

But praying's kind of like riding a bicycle. It comes back to you. I knelt in church while the priest said his prayers and said one of my own, asking God to deal with Armand DuBois as quickly as possible. I had no idea what Armand's agenda was and whether or not it could include offing a few more old ladies—namely my grandmother and my great-aunts. He needed to be stopped, and I prayed that he be stopped quickly.

Driving Me-Maw home to her house, I said, "Secrets have a way of escalating, Me-Maw. They fester and grow and become putrid."

"What you talking about?" she demanded.

"I'm talking about Aunt Blanche. And Armand DuBois. I think Aunt Laurina should know that I know, don't you? She needs to know the secret is finally out in the open."

Me-Maw sat rigidly in the passenger seat, staring straight ahead of her out the windshield. "Ain't nothing out in the open, girl. I tole you not to talk about this none. I tole you that."

"A scab never heals if it never sees the light of day," I said.

"You going to medical school or something? I don't like talking about scabs."

"Me-Maw, all I'm saying is that it would be healthier all around if you and Aunt Adele and Aunt Laurina discussed this. Have you ever talked about it, the three of you?"

"What's to talk about? The past is the past."

"The past also affects our present—"

"Well, thank you kindly, Miz Oprah," Me-Maw said.

"How old was Laurina when all this happened?"

Me-Maw shrugged her shoulders. "I dunno. Seventeen, maybe."

"Don't you think this confused her? Upset her? Did you ever tell her what really happened? Or did you talk about it at all?"

Me-Maw let out an exasperated sigh. "I only told you that 'cause you paw-paw said I needed to. I didn't have no plans of hashing and rehashing the story over and over."

"Me-Maw, I'm worried about Aunt Laurina."

By this time I'd reached Me-Maw's driveway. I pulled in and put the Chevy in park. "Don't turn off the engine," Me-Maw said. "You paw-paw expecting you."

With that she got out of the car without another word and headed for her door. Stubborn old woman.

When I got back to Paw-Paw's shack under the bridge, Pucci was sitting at the table with the two old men, learning how to play forty-two.

Without saying more than a quick "hello," I slipped into Paw-Paw's bedroom and changed out of my Sunday-go-to-meetings and into short shorts and a halter top. The shorts were loose and the halter-top tie was longer than usual. I was losing weight from all the heat and sweating.

I went into the kitchen and started pulling food out of the refrigerator. There wasn't much.

"I'm hungry," I whined.

"Learn to cook, *cher*," Paw-Paw said.

"Maybe I'll go into town. See if I can find some fast-food place close by."

Ho said something in Vietnamese to Paw-Paw, who said, "Ho he say he got a big bunch of *ga xao sa ot* his daughter-in-law sent over. Wanna go eat that? It smell bad but it taste good."

The men put their dominoes up and we traipsed over to Ho's for *ga xao sa ot,* which I couldn't even begin to pronounce. Paw-Paw was half right: It smelled bad. Whether or not it tasted good I have no way of telling; it was so hot with spices, the only flavor I tasted was the Diet Coke I washed it down with. But it was filling.

"Me-Maw tells me they exhumed Cousin Leticia's body Friday," I said to the table in general.

Pucci nodded his head. "Um-hum," he said.

"You knew this?" I asked.

"Um-hum," he said.

"And you didn't tell me?"

Pucci looked at me and raised the dreaded eyebrow. "I'm sorry, Kimmey. Am I supposed to check in with you on a daily or hourly basis?"

"Go to hell," I muttered into my *ga xao sa ot.*

That was the most we'd communicated since Wednesday.

Chapter 13

I DROVE PAW-PAW BACK TO THE DOCTOR'S MONDAY MORNING. HE was getting a short cast, which meant basically that the new cast would be shorter than the old cast. It also meant that he could bend his knee, something I had to help him do, the doctor said, on a daily basis. Rotate, bend, flex, rotate, bend, flex. He would have more mobility, the doctor said, and more range of motion, but he was to stay on the crutches at least until the next visit, one week from then, and maybe even longer.

Another week. I sighed. Could I take another week of this crap? I wondered.

Paw-Paw tuned the radio on the Chevy to his favorite station, a Cajun music station out of Lake Charles, Louisiana. What we called zydeco music in Austin, and in the rest of the world, Paw-Paw called "chankiank."

"Dey's a man right here in Port Arthur makes them concertinas," Paw-Paw said. "Takes a year because each reed got two tones, real small, like eight-to-ten inches, little bitty keys, ever one makes two different sounds. Not many peoples can learn how to play the concertina. Gotta be damned good to play the concertina."

"Gee," I said, my true rock-and-roll self showing through, "all that trouble to sound like that."

"Poo-ee, girl, you don't know good music when you hear it, I tell you what."

We argued about musical merit for a few minutes while Paw-Paw directed me to his favorite out-to-eat spot.

Paw-Paw wasn't much for eating out—always worried he'd use the wrong fork, or burp, so it wasn't surprising, really, that his favorite seafood place was outside on the water, the tables covered with newspaper and shaded by old beach umbrellas. The menu consisted of crabs. That was it. They brought a big tub of steamed crab claws and a basket of French fries and two bottles of Diet Coke. We went through two tubs, three baskets, and four bottles. It was a nice way to spend a hot afternoon.

On the way home, with the radio still tuned to Paw-Paw's favorite station, the newsman came on giving new directions for the disturbance in the Gulf—the former tropical storm George, now once again upgraded—this time to hurricane.

"Oo-ee, I don't like them naming storms after men, I tell you what," Paw-Paw said. "In the old days, them hurrkins and such was named after women, like they supposed to be. Nothing do more damage than a hurrkin or a woman," he said and giggled.

I hit him on the arm. "You old chauvinist," I said. "Ve have vays of making you toe ze line, man person."

"Yeah, little girl, I can't wait till we get this storm, see who you come hide behind when it hit!"

"Ha," I said, flexing my minuscule muscles and doing my best, or worst, Bert Lahr cowardly lion imitation, "I'd like to see it try!"

"You ever been in a hurrkin, girl?"

I shook my head. "No, and I'd just as soon keep my record clean, if you don't mind."

"Well, last I heard it were headin' for Louisiana, but, 'pending on what part of Louisiana, we might get us some."

I felt my stomach begin to knot up. "Will it be bad?"

Paw-Paw shrugged his scrawny shoulders. "Not like it used to be 'fore tracking got so good. Back in fifty-seven, hurrikin Audrey, we been tole all day she were heading for Louisiana but she stalled. When a hurrkin stalls it builds up and turns most times.

"We'd been getting some squalls most of the morning but around noon, it done started hitting the other side of the house. That's when you know the hurrkin done turned and it's coming. So me and you me-maw we got you mama and you Aunt Sylvia—they the only ones still to home—all up and dressed and 'course the Texas Company calls me to come to work 'cause that's what I do and you uncle Lester come over and get you me-maw and the young 'uns and take 'em to the shelter they set up at the school. Well, you me-maw, being the woman she is, the eye come and she say she ain't keeping her young 'uns at the school if she don't have to and she take 'em on back to the house. Now everbody know the back side of a hurrkin the wrong side to be on. Lester call me say Genevieve go back home so I leave the refinery—still in the eye, calm as can be—and get home.

"Then the back side hit and you think all hell done broke loose. Good thing we was home though, 'cause we got 'bout eighteen inches of water in the house from ole Audrey and me and you me-maw and all the children spend the hole day with mops and buckets and rags and stacking furniture so it don't get wet." He sighed. "That was some fun, old Audrey. That was back before they had' the levee and the surge it come in over Pleasure Island and across the Inner Coast Canal and hit Cameron, Looziana, like a freight train. Kilt three or four hunnard people and they be searching for bodies for days."

"Paw-Paw," I said, "this isn't a fun discussion."

"Oh, hell girl, the levee break the surge most time nowdays. But the thing about the surge is it washes the snakes up—the ground rattlers and the freshwater moccasins—they don't like that salty water none. It makes 'em sick, so they crawl up on anything they can find."

"Paw-Paw, I don't like snake stories—"

"Ah, hell, girl, this one ole man in Louisiana, he climb a tree when the water come up high with his little grandbaby and had to break limbs off the tree to whip them snakes off him and the grandbaby all night long. They be crawling up there to get away from the water, just like people—"

I pulled into the driveway of the shack. "Not another word about snakes," I said, slamming on the brakes. "I'm not gonna sleep tonight as it is."

Paw-Paw grinned. "Ah, hell, girl, them holes in the screens ain't big enough for a snake to get through. I don't think."

I shot him a look that could paralyze a lesser man and helped him up the porch steps into the house.

The phone was ringing as I opened the door. I rushed inside and picked it up.

"Hello?" I said.

"Kimmey?"

"Will?"

"My mother's autopsy has been completed," he said.

I held my breath.

"You were right," he said.

* * *

After getting Paw-Paw settled and fed (after the feast that afternoon a quick bowl of canned soup seemed to do the trick), I got in the car and raced to Will's apartment. To say he was upset on the phone was like saying Dorisca Judice was a flirt. Understatement City. He'd asked me to come over, telling me he'd let me know the results of the autopsy when I got there. I didn't mention any of this to Pucci. I wasn't sure I'd be able to find him—but then again, I didn't look. I figured he already had the information from Buddy Don. I thought I'd like a little info of my own. And from my own source. Not to mention I'd like to think Will didn't hate me anymore. There was always that.

The first squall hit while I was driving over to Will's apartment. A quick little shower. Nothing for a landlubber like Kimmey Kruse to get excited about. It cooled things off. Made the earth smell fresh.

I rang the bell on Will's apartment door and he opened it as if he'd been standing there with his eye to the peephole. As bloodshot as the eye was, there was that possibility. But I feared the real reason was that Will had been crying. Personally, I find that very attractive in a man.

I touched my hand to his cheek and led him to the sofa, where we both sat down.

"Will—"

"You were right all along, Kimmey." He teared up. It made his eyes sparkle and my heart bleed. "Mama had been drugged. Seconal, I think they said. A sleeping pill."

"He must have gotten it into her Big Red somehow," I said, musing. "Maybe Dorisca was supposed to do that. She'd do anything he said, probably, not knowing he was going to kill her—"

I stopped when I saw the pain in Will's face. He stood up

and walked to a window, his back to me. I stood, following him to the window, where I put my hand lightly on his back.

"Will, I'm sorry. I'm so sorry."

He turned and I took the huge, over-six-foot man into my arms, his head resting on my shoulder, his body racking with sobs. I held him tight, cooing to him and rubbing his back with both my hands. His sobs subsided, but he didn't move his head—except to nuzzle my neck. His hands, which had been around my waist, moved to my buttocks, pushing my body up against an erection the size of Dallas. One hand found its way under my loose shirt while his mouth found mine. The hand under my shirt discovered I wasn't wearing a bra and his fingers began rubbing the nipple.

Curiously enough, my mind seemed to be occupied with two thoughts. One was that the last time I'd had sex there'd been *coitus interruptus* in a big way—the guy had dropped dead on me. The second thought was that my body didn't seem to be half as turned on by all this manipulation as it had been by that one little tongueless kiss with Pucci.

I gently pulled away. "Will, do you think now—"

"Yes!" he said, pulling me back to him, holding me tightly, his hands pulling at my shirt, his mouth sucking at my neck.

"He's gorgeous," I told myself. "He's sweet," I told myself. Still, nothing happened.

I pushed him away firmly and moved out of his reach. "Why don't you try miniature golf or bowling?" I said.

"What?" he demanded.

"If you want to take your mind off your troubles, that would work just as well. I'd rather not be used as just a mental block."

He reached out his hand for me but I backed up. "Kimmey," he said, "you know it's more than that."

I sighed. "Let's get all this behind us, Will, and then we'll talk about . . . us."

His face turned hard. "You know, I thought you were someone I could turn to in my grief, but I guess I was wrong."

"No, Will. You were right. If you want to talk about it, fine. I'll try to help you work it all out. But I don't think sex is the answer to your problems."

He walked to the door and opened it. "Thanks, but no thanks," he said.

I picked up my bag and left. I wasn't doing too well in the men department lately. And that's the truth.

The little squall I'd encountered on my way to Will's had turned into a full-blown storm as I headed back to the bridge. I turned on the radio to see how bad it was, tuning in to a local Port Arthur station, only to find out we were getting the edge of hurricane George, which had just slammed into a mostly deserted area of Louisiana near the Texas border. By the time I reached the bridge, the waters of the river were churning like crazy, swells crashing against the docks. I drove as fast as possible to Paw-Paw's shack.

The pundits had been saying the hurricane would slam into Mexico, and its course early on certainly seemed to indicate that. But George had made a turn sometime in the wee hours of that morning and had been making a beeline for New Orleans most of the day.

While New Orleanians had been battening down the hatches, George changed course again, and about an hour ago had come ashore between Grand Chenier and Cameron, traveling inland as far as Gibbstown and Armentine.

Ho, Pucci, and Paw-Paw were busy tying down everything that was too big to move into the shack or the Scenic Cruiser. The entire marina area was abuzz with people battening down their own hatches or helping their neighbors batten down theirs—those who weren't already in their cars and heading out of the marina to higher ground. The shrimpers and other boaters were busy tying down their boats or, if they were small enough, bringing them on shore for protection.

In the few moments it took me to notice all this, the wind had picked up, gusting to such a degree that an unprotected peacock came flying past my car window, and to the best of my knowledge, peacocks don't fly.

I jumped out of the car and asked Paw-Paw what I could do.

"Go in the camp and load up some clothes and such. You me-maw said for us to come on to her place. It be higher there. You got time, fill up some jugs with water if the pump still work. Be some clean plastic milk jugs under the sink in the kitchen. That where my hurrkin box is—it got flashlights and extra batteries and whatnot—you bring that with them clothes, *ti-cher*, yeah?"

I hurried into the shack, taking a peek at Pucci as I passed. He seemed particularly pale, and I made note of the fact that this sissy boy was from Chicago and didn't know from a hurricane. Okay, so I was raised in Austin, somewhat inland itself, but I'd heard hurricane stories at my mother's knee since the beginning of time and was somewhat prepared for it. Well, maybe not—considering the wind that was tearing at my clothes and the rain that was lashing down like a hard shower spray—but I could pretend.

I grabbed the hurricane box, and while the first plastic milk jug filled with water, I grabbed a suitcase and began stuffing it with essentials for Paw-Paw and myself. After I'd filled three milk jugs, I lugged everything outside.

The wind tore the door from my hand and I spilled one of the jugs before Pucci ran up and helped me. He looked at me and said, "I'd rather face the Mafia than this."

I smiled weakly and tried my best to move toward Pucci's rental. With Pucci's help, we both got there and got in the car. Pucci got behind the wheel, with Ho and me taking up the back seat and Paw-Paw riding shotgun, giving instructions on how best to get out of the marina and head for higher ground.

"You me-maw say we come on over to her house," Paw-Paw said. "We was gonna go a while back but we was worried about you, girl. Where you been?"

"Finding out about Cousin Leticia's autopsy," I said loudly, shooting a look at Pucci. He didn't seem interested, however, in anything other than the trees along the marina road, which were bent almost double in the wind.

I figured we were lucky with Paw-Paw's short cast. It gave him more mobility to move quickly. And it looked as if we just might have to do that.

Pucci started the car and backed out of the oystershell driveway. The blacktop road, which was usually mostly potholes, was now mostly lake, and Pucci drove slowly, the wake behind the car big enough to water-ski on.

When we got to the entrance to the highway, there wasn't a car in sight going our way. A bumper-to-bumper line of cars was going over the bridge heading north toward Orange, but we had no trouble going south before we turned west into the Groves.

The main roads of the Groves were congested with traffic trying to get out of the city, so Paw-Paw gave Pucci back-street directions to get to Me-Maw's. The side streets to Me-Maw's house were low and full of water. We made it to within three blocks of Me-Maw's when Pucci hit a puddle that was more like Lake Pontchartrain and the rental stalled out.

The rain was coming down in sheets now and the wind was buffeting the car like rioters after an NBA play-off. We were several miles inland from the canal, but still the storm raged as if we were standing on the beach.

"What do we do now?" Pucci yelled over the sound and fury of the storm. "We can't go out in this, can we?"

Pucci was terrified. I could tell by the whiteness of his lips and his death grip on the steering wheel of the car. I reached over and touched his hand where it gripped the wheel. He took my hand in his and squeezed. I thought for a minute my hand would break. But it was still somehow reassuring.

"We gotta wait," Paw-Paw shouted back. "The eye it be coming soon, I betja."

He'd no more than said it when the rain began to slack off. The wind began to slow. Within ten minutes, the wind was gone and the rain was nothing more than a fine drizzle. The sky was a curious yellow-black. The houses around us let off a strange yellow light—not electric light but kerosene light. Obviously the electricity had gone with the wind.

We all got out of the car and stood, staring at the sky. The air was deathly still. The trees, which only moments before had been bent double by the wind, now had not one leaf stirring. The quiet was deafening after the rage of the storm. Somehow, this seemed even scarier—like standing on a movie set for a "day after" film.

"We got at most an hour," Paw-Paw said. "We best get on to Genevieve's house."

We decided to leave the stuff in the trunk of the car and, against his protests, Pucci and Ho picked Paw-Paw up in a fireman's carry. We made the three blocks to Me-Maw's house in less than five minutes.

She was standing on the porch when we walked up to her yard.

"Oo-eeee, you peoples get in here now, yeah? You look like drowned rats. Come on, now," Me-Maw said, her eyes on the sky as she waved us forward.

Forty minutes after we got into Me-Maw's kitchen, warming our bellies with crawfish *ettoufee* and shrimp bisque, the eye passed over, bringing the other half of the storm on us. And, as Paw-Paw had said, this side was a lot nastier than the front. The old frame house rocked on its pier-and-beam foundation, and a window crashed out in one of the back bedrooms. Pucci and I ran in, grabbing a blanket off the bed and securing it to the window with a staple gun, wondering how many minutes it would hold.

While we were in the bedroom, a loud crash from the back of the house had us running into the kitchen, where Me-Maw, Paw-Paw, and Ho stood looking out the back door.

"Well, never was too sturdy to begin with, Genevieve," Paw-Paw said, staring at the detached one-car garage that lay sideways in the yard.

"I don't care 'bout that stupid ole' garage," Me-Maw said, her arms crossed over her bosom, her stern look on her face, "it just had all you old junk in it. But that damned thing fell on my tomato plants!"

"Like those tomato plants was even still there! *Poo-au-ee,* Genevieve. 'Sides, you tomatoes always get mealy anyhow."

"Who say my tomatoes mealy?" Me-Maw demanded in a loud voice, drowning out the raging storm.

"Everbody know you tomatoes mealy. It the talk a Port Arthur," Paw-Paw shouted.

"Well, at least I could grow 'em, Tobert Broussard. You never growed anything in you life!"

"I growed me eight daughters!" Paw-Paw shouted. "That ain't half bad, yeah, Genevieve?"

To my surprise, Me-Maw laughed, hitting Paw-Paw on the arm. "Tobert, you a scoundrel!"

Paw-Paw grinned at Me-Maw. "That what you like, yeah, Genevieve?"

Me-Maw blushed, giggled, and moved to the stove.

"Y'all come on and eat some this food 'fore it go bad," Me-Maw said. She didn't have to tell me twice.

Paw-Paw and Ho took the twin beds in the guest bedroom, leaving Me-Maw her own king-sized bed in her own bedroom. The third bedroom was Me-Maw's sewing room (complete with all the necessary equipment to make me a balloon-and-ribbon-adorned T-shirt just exactly like Norvella's, if I so chose—I have to think about it, I said. Yeah, right); it had no sleeping quarters in it. Which left Pucci and me sharing the Early American couch and/or floor.

After everyone had gone to bed, we sat together on the couch talking about the case, Cousin Will, the possibility of working my family into a really good routine (major funny stuff), anything and everything, except us. He spent a lot of that time with the tips of his fingers running through what little there was of my hair and I spent a majority of that time with phrases from bad romance novels going through my mind. You know, things like, "The storm raged and so did I." Or, "The thunder erupted as our passions rose."

His fingers had a way of making my mind blank, so that our conversation was a little disjointed:

Pucci: "You think we'll find Armand DuBois?"

Me: "Um."

Pucci: "You think your cousin Will's still mad at you?"

Me: "Ooo."

Pucci: "Can you do the Cajun accent well enough for a routine?"

Me: "Ahhhh."

At some point, the storm petered out and so did I. I fell asleep.

I awoke in Pucci's arms. There was a very large part of me that declared that this was not at all a bad place to wake up. There was another part of me that shook off that larger part like a Labrador retriever shaking off river water. All that shaking, unfortunately, woke Pucci up.

"Good morning," he said, smiling at me.

My longest live-in relationship, Billy from during and right after college, used to wake up with what he called a "piss-hard" every morning. Billy was of the firm opinion, shared, I'm sure, by most men, that there's a finite number of erections in any man's life, and none is to be wasted. The smile I was getting from Pucci led me to believe he was of that school of thought.

The banging from the kitchen, Me-Maw obviously preparing breakfast, dissuaded any ideas Pucci may have had and had me moving quickly into the bathroom to wash up and go help. Cooking was preferable to being leered at by an Italian cop.

After breakfast, Pucci and I walked outside to the apparent aftermath of World War III. At least that's what it looked like. Branches and whole trees were down, blocking roads; people's doors lying on roofs and tangled in downed power lines and telephone poles.

Port Arthur, Texas, was blessed with billboards lying across freeways and the caved-in roof of the K-Mart (causing general panic in a K-Mart-shopping town). The hospitals, police stations, and the evacuee centers were the only places with electricity.

We river rats—Paw-Paw, Ho, Pucci, and I, were used to roughing it, but with the blazing sun and the unbelievably high humidity of the day after, Me-Maw spent most of her time bemoaning the loss of her central air-conditioning and fanning herself with whatever came to hand.

The phone service was also out, so we spent a great deal of the day feeding relatives who came by to "check up" on Me-Maw—everyone knowing her quickly thawing deep-freeze goodies would be available to all.

By seven o'clock that night, we had twenty-seven people in the house, most of them women, and all of them cooking spoilage from the freezer over Me-Maw's gas stove. The men started the barbecue in the backyard (after they found it under some debris) and I sat around trying to work my relatives into an act without getting into too much trouble. I could do Me-Maw's voice, but Norvella's voice was going to take some work. Possibly surgery on my vocal cords.

Around eight o'clock, there was a knock on the door. I was the closest to it and went to answer it. Barbara Sue stood on Me-Maw's stoop in her hurricane outfit: designer jeans tucked into bejeweled turquoise cowboy boots, and a ruffled western shirt in a pattern of grazing cows. A turquoise cowboy hat was perched on top of her head, pinned up Australian-style with a gold cross pin. She did her air-kiss routine and said, "Everybody all right here?"

"Just fine. You hungry?" I asked. "We seem to be feeding everybody in a five-block radius. Might as well join us."

"Oh, I couldn't eat a bite. I just thought it was my Christian duty to come check up on my kin and make sure everybody survived the storm okay."

"How'd you get through all the high water . . ." I started, then said, "Oh, your Blazer . . ."

Barbara Sue cocked her head smartly and smiled. "How'd you know about my Jezebel? That's what I call my Blazer."

Oops. Well, why not? I thought, and opened the screen door, stepping out on the porch with Barbara Sue. I sat down on the top step and patted the space next to me. "Have a seat, Barbara Sue," I said, smiling sweetly.

She sat down next to me, her head still cocked cutely my way. I wondered if she'd get a crick in her neck if she didn't straighten it soon.

I sighed, wondering how to bring this up. But since I was rapidly becoming less than fond of my former favorite cousin, I thought blurting it out would work as well as anything else.

"I saw you get in the Blazer the other day at the strip shopping center over on Twelfth Street," I said. "I'm working over there part-time," I said.

"Oh?" Her smile was weakening.

"You got out of Will DuBois's car and got into yours."

"Oh," she said, her head no longer cocked but held erect and staring straight ahead of her.

"I understand you and Will used to date in college," I said.

"Briefly," she said.

I sighed. "Barbara Sue, something's going on and, since there have been a couple of murders lately, I'd really like to know what it is."

Barbara Sue sucked in her breath and turned to stare at me. "Murder? Why, goodness gracious, who's been murdered?"

Where have you been? I thought but instead said, "Cousin Leticia and a woman named Dorisca Judice. They're connected."

"Cousin Leticia was murdered?" Barbara Sue exclaimed, with a little too much innocence for my taste.

"Yes, dear, Cousin Leticia was murdered. And you said something to the effect, 'She better not have told anyone' to Will when you got out of his car. Who is 'she,' and what was it she wasn't supposed to tell?"

Barbara Sue stood up. "Why, I have no idea what you are

talking about, Kimberly Anne," she said, a sweet smile on her face. It was still there when she said, "But God doesn't like snoops. Remember that." She marched down the steps and out into the street where the Blazer was parked in mid-wheel water.

Interesting, I thought.

I went back inside and up to Cousin Norvella, who was busily telling Pucci about a recent gallbladder operation her mother had experienced. I'd noticed Norvella's big Dodge van parked near Barbara Sue's Blazer. Obviously a vehicle that could negotiate the flooded streets as well as Barbara Sue's.

"I need to borrow the keys to your van," I told Norvella.

"Oh, Kimberly, did I tell you what a terrible time Mama had when they pulled her gallbladder?"

"Yes, you did, Norvella. Just awful. But a wonderful story. I know Pucci'd love to hear every detail. But I have an emergency—"

"Oh, goodness," Norvella said, the voice echoing up and down my spine, "can I help?"

"No, no, just let me borrow your van—"

"What's the emergency?" Pucci asked, obviously eager to help out if it meant getting away from Norvella and her mother's gallbladder.

"We're out of red sauce," I said.

Norvella handed me the keys. "That sure is an emergency," she said. I hightailed it out of there and into Norvella's van.

Barbara Sue was long gone, but I had a hunch where she might be headed. I drove straight to Will's apartment complex, navigating the high-water streets like a pro. When I reached Will's apartment-complex parking lot, I saw the Chevy Blazer parked in Visitor's Parking. I hid Norvella's van at the far end of the lot, making sure there were several cars between it and the Blazer. Getting out, I ran down to Barbara Sue's car and opened the passenger-side door. As I'd hoped, she'd been in too much of a hurry to lock the doors.

I scooted down in the seat and waited. Fifteen minutes later the dome light came on in the Blazer as Barbara Sue opened the door. She stopped dead, half in and half out of the car, when she saw me.

I smiled. "Hop in," I said. "We need to talk some turkey."

Chapter

14

"GET OUT OF MY CAR, KIMBERLY ANNE, AND GET OUT OF MY LIFE!"
she said, getting in and slamming the door. "Now! Get out!"

I smiled and shook my head. "No way."

"Willard told me what all you've been up to. If it weren't
for you, nobody'd even care if that old biddy got herself murdered. You didn't know her, Kimmey. You didn't! She was
a . . . a . . . witch!"

"Good Christian lady like that?"

Barbara Sue leaned her head against the steering wheel
and began to sob. And I began to feel bad. I'm not cut out for
this sort of thing, I told myself. I patted her on the back.

"Barbara Sue, I'm sorry, I really am—"

"No, you're not! If you were sorry you'd go away and leave
me in peace!"

"Two women are dead, Barbara Sue. Are you responsi-
ble?"

"What?" She jerked her head away from the steering

wheel and stared at me. And what a sight she was. Tammy Faye, move over.

"What was going on between you and Leticia?"

Barbara Sue leaned her head against the headrest and sighed. "This is none of your business—"

"If it proves to have nothing to do with the murders, then it won't go any further than this car."

She turned and looked at me. "I used to like you," she said.

"Yeah, I used to like you, too. I used to look up to you."

Barbara Sue smiled. "Yeah. I remember. You were the only person who ever did. I loved you for that." She leaned her head back again and let out another sigh. "Remember how wild I was?"

"Yes," I said. "Like a young colt, I always thought. Full of life."

She laughed. "Well, that was nothing compared to when I got to Lamar. Really let my hair down once I got away from home." She lifted her head and looked at me. "I had my way with every single member of the Kappa Alpha Fraternity. Alphabetically."

"Alphabetically?"

She grinned. "At least it was systematic."

"True," I said, grinning back.

"Willard was a KA."

"Ah," I said.

"A *D,*" she said. "DuBois. I didn't even know we were related the first time we were together. Then, when he said he was from Armentine and I mentioned my family having come from there, well, we worked out that we were kin."

"Scary, huh?"

She leaned her head back again. "No. It wasn't. I liked it. We weren't related enough for it to make a difference either morally or legally." She laughed. "Not that morality was high on my list at that time. But the connection—I liked that. So we started seeing each other. I exaggerated. I only went to the *H*'s. Didn't have my way with the entire fraternity, although that had been my plan. I stopped with Jasper Hebert." She shuddered. "He could cure even the most dedicated nympho. Nasty guy. Anyway, Willard and I started going together, even though his brother KAs gave him a pretty hard time about it. You know, the fraternity round heel."

I touched her hand and she held mine, squeezing it slightly. "I fell in love. After a fashion. And got pregnant. The doctor said I was two months along and I had finished with Jasper Hebert four months before. So it was definitely Willard's baby. But he didn't believe me. I begged him to marry me. Begged him. So he left school. I went by the KA house one day to see him and they said he was gone. Bag and baggage. A week later he came back—with Leticia.

"She came to my dorm and asked to take me to lunch. I thought, great, this is Me-Maw's cousin. She'll do the right thing. She'll make Willard marry me." Barbara Sue laughed bitterly. "Oh, yeah. We get to the restaurant and order and the food comes. I'm starving. After all, I'm pregnant. I'm stuffing this burger down my throat when Leticia hands me a sheet of paper. It's legal-sized, notarized and everything. And it said—I remember every word of that piece of paper—'I, the undersigned, do solemnly swear that I had carnal knowledge of Barbara Sue Bingham during the fall semester of 1976.' It was signed by *every* member of the fraternity. Even the *I*'s and the *S*'s and the *T*'s." I squeezed her hand and she looked at me. "Remember, I was only two months pregnant."

I nodded my head.

"Strange things happen to a woman during early pregnancy." She looked at me and grinned. "I puked that hamburger all over that sweet Christian lady."

I laughed out loud, and Barbara Sue laughed with me. My old Barbara Sue. The cousin of my childhood.

She sighed again and leaned her head back. "So—I left school. I called my parents and told them I'd run off with some guy, knowing they'd buy that, and I went to this home this friend of mine told me about in Kansas. An unwed mother's home." She looked at me and shook her head. "I know, I coulda had an abortion. But remember, I was raised Catholic. It never even entered my head. I had the baby—a girl—I saw her for all of two minutes." Barbara Sue sighed. "She was beautiful. Just like Willard. Black hair, pale skin. Blue eyes. Oh, what a picture she was!"

I patted Barbara Sue's hand and she looked at me. "They took her away to be adopted. This was before birth mothers routinely got to meet the adoptive parents. I have no idea to this day where she is or how she's doing. My 16-year-old daughter. But every September twelfth I find some time to be by myself and I sing my little girl the 'Happy Birthday' song. I call her Melissa. That's what I would have named her."

I reached over and hugged her. I couldn't help myself. "I didn't kill Leticia," Barbara Sue said. "But if wishes could kill, she'd a been a dead woman long ago."

"Does your husband know about this?"

She sighed. "No. And he's not going to. Do you understand that, Kimberly?"

"If this has nothing to do with Leticia's murder, then he won't."

"It doesn't."

I wanted to say I believed her. But I couldn't.

I got back to Me-Maw's house around ten to find a fighting-mad Norvella.

"So where's the red sauce?" she demanded. "I tole Me-

Maw what you said and she said she had plenty of red sauce! You are so weird, Kimberly Anne!"

With that she grabbed her keys and headed out the door. I noticed no one begged her to stay.

Ten minutes after I got back, Me-Maw pulled me aside as I was preparing to begin on my third course of food for the evening. "I jest hear on the portable radio that Armentine be flooded real bad. Me and Adele we go to Armentine tomorrow try to do something 'bout Leticia's things. Her house be flooded maybe. We gotta go see. You wanna go?"

To Armentine? To the start of everything that had happened here? You bet your butt I did.

Nothing's easy. Paw-Paw decided he wanted to go to Armentine, too. And where Paw-Paw went, it seemed Ho was sure to follow. Pucci thought it would be nice to see Louisiana, as long as we were going and since he'd never been there.

Since none of the cars would sit six comfortably, Pucci took his rental back to the airport and exchanged it for a twelve-passenger van. That gave Paw-Paw and his broken leg plenty of room, Aunt Adele and Ho sat together on the long back bench seat, and Me-Maw had the middle one all to herself. I sat up front with Pucci. Me-Maw, of course, was sharing her seat with the picnic hamper and ice chest. Lest somebody get hungry. I agreed there was always that chance.

Armentine was straight east of Port Arthur, but because of the floods we decided to stick to the bigger roads and headed north up 87 to Orange, where we took Highway 90 into Louisiana, then went south on 27. It was incredible how the road changed the minute we got into Louisiana—from 1990s freeway travel to 1920s backwoods roads.

We seemed to be all coupled up—with Me-Maw and Paw-

Paw giggling away in their separate seats, Paw-Paw turned sideways to entertain my grandmother better, and Adele and Ho talking up a storm in some obscure form of French they both seemed to understand.

I, of course, had Pucci. "What do you get when you have a cow with Alzheimer's?" he asked.

"Do you save these up to torture me?" I asked. "You write them down and memorize them late at night? Have them on a computer listing somewhere? Subscribe to a bad-joke hot line? What?"

"Milk of amnesia."

"I'm not laughing—"

He grinned. "Oh, but you have! Okay, what do you call a rich Irishman who lives outside all the time?"

"Pucci, I'm not listening to you. I'm staring outside at the beautiful scenery—"

"Paddy O'Furniture," he said, laughing like an idiot.

"What's that, Bo?" Paw-Paw called from the seat behind him. So, naturally, Pucci repeated that joke and the cow joke, which started Paw-Paw up on a joke, which reminded Me-Maw of a joke, to which she'd naturally forgotten the punch line, and on and on. I counted Spanish moss clumps.

After the jokes subsided, Paw-Paw began telling stories about the *feu-follet*, a ball of fire which the old Cajuns believed was the mysterious fire brought on by the lonely wanderer. Whoever he was. If a *feu-follet* was seen near a house, it portended death.

"Oo-eee," Paw-Paw said, "they say you see a *feu-follet*, you cow she gonna go dry. My uncle Adras he seen a *feu-follet*, next thing he know his horse he got twisted knots in his tail."

Me-Maw took up the tale, her voice low for maximum effect. "They say the *feu-follet* it really the soul of the restless spirit of a unbaptized baby. That why, when Blanche's baby die in childbirth, we had the priest over and had that baby baptized quick-like." She shuddered. "That *feu-follet,* some say it just michievous, me, I say it evil."

I turned around in my seat. "Me-Maw, you don't really believe in that, do you?"

Me-Maw shot me her mean look. "Girl, they more to this world than what you jest see and know. The world of the spirits ain't always so nice."

I sighed. "Me-Maw, Daddy says a *feu-follet* is nothing more than a ball of marsh gas. Just decaying vegetation. Like Saint Elmo's fire—it has a perfectly rational explanation."

The three old Cajuns exchanged glances with each other, and Paw-Paw said, "Whatever you say, girl. You believe you daddy if you want to, yeah? Me, I stay away from the *feu-follet!*"

I turned around and Pucci and I drove on in silence after that, with the old people whispering and giggling in the back. I tried not to think they were talking about me, but I knew better.

I thought about my cousin Barbara Sue and what she'd told me the night before. And I thought about the fun-loving, mischief-making cousin I'd known as a child, compared to the uptight, anal-retentive, overly dressed cousin I now knew. Could she commit murder? Could she cold-bloodedly, premeditatively kill Cousin Leticia to keep her own dark secret from her self-righteous, holier-than-thou husband?

Armentine, Louisiana, usually surrounded by bayous and swamps, was now a swamp itself. We were lucky to be in the van, as a regular car might not have made it into the little town at all.

Me-Maw directed Pucci to Cousin Leticia's house, two blocks off the main street of town. It was a little white clapboard house on a pier-and-beam foundation. The street in front of Leticia's house was knee-deep in water and the water was lapping lazily at Leticia's front door. I doubted it had to knock to get in.

We all piled out of the van, wading to Leticia's front door, with Ho and Pucci doing the fireman's carry again with Paw-Paw, in an attempt to keep his short cast out of the water.

"Oo-eee, it gonna stink in here," Me-Maw said.

After he'd been deposited on the porch, Paw-Paw said to Pucci, "Bo, you go round the back, check see the electricity it turned off, yeah? We don't wanna go 'lectricuting our butts, yeah?"

The house wasn't locked. It wasn't as if Cousin Leticia had planned to be gone for more than a day. The water was less than an inch deep in the worst spots in the living room, but it was apparent from the stains on the walls that it had been higher the day before.

Me-Maw had packed flattened boxes into the van and rolls of tape. It was my job to find a dry spot and re-erect the boxes. This I did on the kitchen table while Me-Maw and Aunt Adele began picking up priceless heirlooms: a salt-and-pepper-shaker set Cousin Leticia's mama had bought on a trip to Atlanta back in 1934; a round butter dish Me-Maw said Cousin Leticia should have never gotten from their mutual grandmother in the first place—it was supposed to have gone to Me-Maw, not Leticia; a ceramic mushroom Adele was certain Leticia had bought when she was with her on a trip to the store back during their first year of high school, et cetera.

Paw-Paw sat on the semi-soaked sofa, his foot propped on the coffee table, directing Ho and Pucci on what to do with the bigger items. "Y'all take that stereo system. If Will don't want it, I can use it at the camp." Or, "Oo-eee, lookee that rocker. You think it dry out enough ever use again? Probably. Y'all put it over there, we get it in the van."

After I got the boxes put back together, Pucci and I went

exploring the bedrooms. There was one with a soaked king-sized bed and smaller dresser taking up the entire room, another with sewing supplies, much like Me-Maw's house, except with no extra room for company. The bedroom offered no clues as to the whereabouts of Leticia's husband. There were a Bible, a Bible study book, and a Bible story book on the bedside table. A picture of a blond, blue-eyed Jesus stared down from the wall over the bed.

The top dresser drawer held neat piles of underwear, hosiery, slips, et cetera. The middle drawer held entirely too many craft T-shirts. The bottom drawer had been Letitia's desk. In it were stacks of paid bills, a few unpaid bills, none overdue at the time they were sent, several religious tracts, and a large family Bible.

I grabbed it and plopped down on the middle of the king-sized bed and opened it to the family tree on the back. I recognized some names, like my great-great-grandmother and -grandfather, but most of the names were unrecognizable. I looked at Armand DuBois's name nestled next to Leticia's. Branching off from his name were his own ancestors. I wrote some of the names down on an old bill from Cousin Leticia's drawer, thinking it might be a way to trace the elusive Mr. DuBois.

Pucci sat next to me on the bed, watching me work. Just like a man. Finally, he stretched, saying, "Let's get out of here. This house stinks. Literally."

I agreed and we headed into the kitchen, where the troops had all gathered to stare at the contents of Leticia's refrigerator. "We just gotta throw all this stuff out," Me-Maw said.

"Well, hell, girl," Paw-Paw said, "that ketchup look like it be okay."

"You want me to get a box jest so you can take that half-empty bottle of ketchup back to you house? You really that cheap, Tobert?" Me-Maw demanded.

"Don't you talk to me about cheap, Genevieve Foret Broussard! You ain't the one trying to pay for two houses outta one little pension check, yeah!"

"Oh, you begrudging me that house I clean for you and cook in for you ever day for thirty-five year? That what you saying, Tobert?"

"All I saying is I want the ketchup. Can I please have the ketchup, Genevieve?"

Me-Maw threw the half-empty plastic bottle of ketchup at Paw-Paw, who sat at the kitchen table, leg propped up on a chair. He caught it and grinned. "Why, *merci bou coup, cher.* You heart as big as you butt, I do declare."

Me-Maw turned with fire in her eye but then laughed. "Tobert, you be the death of me."

I chose that moment to intervene. "Pucci and I are going outside for a breath of air—"

"Good," Me-Maw said, her head back inside the refrigerator, "go check out that shed in the backyard. See if there anything out there need to be seen to, yeah?"

I started to protest, but Pucci took me by the shoulders and turned me toward the back door. "No problem, Mrs. Broussard. We'll take care of it."

Leticia's property was about two acres, the back higher than the front. The floodwater had receded from the backyard, leaving lines of debris in its wake. The shed stood at the back, sheltered in the corner next to the fence that kept the swamp behind Letitia's property from encroaching on her formerly well-manicured lawn and kept her next-door neighbor's old plow horse from eating her geraniums.

We walked slowly toward the shed, breathing in the fresh air as we did. Pucci reached out for the door handle, only to have the door stick on him. We both worked at it and got it about halfway open. A small window in the side of the shed let in enough light to see the debris. The flood had done its damage. Paint cans had fallen from the lower shelves, the lawn mower was pushed up against the back wall, a bag of lawn clippings had spilled open, leaving a mess on the dirt floor. And then, of course, there was the skeleton in the center of the shed.

"Jesus Christ!" Pucci said, grabbing me and pushing me back toward the door.

"Oh, my God!" I said, pushing him forward to get a better look.

After we stopped shoving each other, Pucci squatted down on the damp earth floor to get a better look at the remains. There wasn't much—bones and a few tattered remnants of cloth. A metal zipper lay near the neck of the skeleton, worked up there probably by the flood waters.

"Who in the hell do you think this is?" Pucci asked, figuratively scratching his head.

I remember once, when I was about eleven or twelve, my mother taking me to the movies to see *Murder on the Orient Express.* It was her desire that I start reading books and she thought if I liked the movie, it might interest me in reading Agatha Christie. It worked. I read every one of her books after that. But that day, at the matinee performance of *Murder on the Orient Express,* a weird thing happened. I was watching the movie intently and about ten minutes before Hercule Poirot made his great denouement, all of Agatha's clues came together for me and I announced to my mother in a loud, high voice, "They all did it!" The evil stares from the other movie patrons were not something I'm fond of remembering.

But that's the feeling I was having as I stood staring down at the skeleton in Cousin Leticia's shed. I knew. Beyond a shadow of a doubt. I knew whose skeleton it was and I knew who had killed Cousin Leticia and Dorisca Judice. And the knowledge scared the crap out of me.

I grabbed Pucci's shoulder. "Let's get out of here!"

He shrugged me off. "Wait a minute—"

"Now!" I screamed. "Now, Pucci!"

He stood up and I pushed him out the door of the shed and ran, dragging him behind me, back to the house.

My family and Ho were still checking out the kitchen when we barged in the back door.

"Let's go!" I shouted.

They all turned and looked at me, not one of them moving. "I said now, people! Get a move on!"

"What come over you, girl?" Paw-Paw asked, sitting next to his half-empty bottle of ketchup, which now shared space with a quarter-empty bottle of Louisiana Redhot, an unopened bottle of picante sauce, and a box of macaroni.

I didn't stop to think what dinner might be that night. I just grabbed Paw-Paw's leg and not so gently dropped it to the floor. "Get up!" I shouted. "Me-Maw, close the damn refrigerator door! All of you come on, we've got to get out of—"

I stopped because Me-Maw was smiling and looking at the door that led into the living room. I looked, too.

"Well, hey, Willard," Me-Maw said. "Glad you could join us."

Will was standing there, his large frame blocking most of the doorway. "Hey, Cousin Genevieve, Cousin Adele." He nodded toward us all.

I smiled. "Hi, Will, we were just leaving—"

"So soon?" he asked, smiling at me.

"Yes, we decided to go get some lunch in town—"

"Oo-eee, girl, I brought a whole basket of food—" Me-Maw started.

"Which, unfortunately, Pucci dropped in the floodwater, didn't you, Pucci, so I thought he could treat us all to lunch at the Dairy Queen. How does that sound?"

I stopped babbling when I saw the large gun in Cousin Will's hand.

Pucci saw it, too. "What the fu——" he started to say, simultaneously taking a step in Cousin Will's direction. He shouldn't have done that, probably. Not a smart thing for a Chicago detective to do. But he did it. Maybe it had something to do with being in a strange place. Being on vacation. Not having his suit on. I don't know. But he did it. He took a step toward Cousin Will. And Cousin Will shot him.

Chapter

15

Everything took on a nightmarish quality. I screamed and fell to my knees next to Pucci—the scream echoing in my ears. The blood was flowing from high on his chest, near the shoulder. The bullet wound itself might not be fatal, I thought, but he could bleed to death. Me-Maw was beside me in an instant, a kitchen towel in her hand, pressing it against the wound. I turned to look at Will—just as Paw-Paw hit him in the face with one of his crutches. Ho, who'd been standing unobtrusively on the other side of the doorway, out of Will's line of sight, seemed to levitate in slow motion, his right leg going out and up and connecting beautifully with Will's balls. Will fell to his knees, but his screams of pain were quickly quieted by Aunt Adele's blow to the head with a cast-iron skillet. Will went down like a lead balloon.

It all happened so quickly I wasn't sure I'd even seen it.

But that wasn't anything I had time to worry about. Picking up Cousin Leticia's telephone did little more than frustrate me further as the lines were down, obviously, from the floods. By mutual agreement, Me-Maw and Aunt Adele and I picked up Pucci and carried him to the van. We laid him out on the back seat while I continued to apply pressure to the wound. Me-Maw and Aunt Adele hovered nearby, telling me exactly how to apply pressure, how to sit, how to hold my mouth, et cetera, while Ho drove us to the nearest hospital, with Paw-Paw directing.

We skidded to a stop in front of the emergency room of the Armentine Memorial Hospital and Me-Maw jumped out and began directing the orderlies and nurses on how to do their job. Within minutes we were all sitting in a little room off the emergency room talking to Sheriff Homer Bullet (pronounced Bu-lea), who'd already directed deputies to go pick up Cousin Will.

"And the truth shall set ye free."

"What?" Sheriff Bullet said, looking at me as if I'd possibly gone nuts.

I looked at Me-Maw. "Those were almost the last words of Cousin Leticia, remember, Me-Maw?"

She nodded. "I remember." She looked at me in confusion. "What be happening, Kimberly? I don't understand."

I took a deep breath. "Sheriff, I think you should call Detective Buddy Don Keehoe of the Port Arthur Police Department and have him come up here. All this is related to a couple of murders down there."

"Oh?" Sheriff Bullet said, leaning his rather large butt against the door of the room. "And you tell me what all this is, yeah?"

"Fifteen years ago, Armand DuBois came calling on his wife and son, our cousin Leticia and her son Will. He'd done it before. Come calling and always ended up beating up Leticia and taking whatever money she had. This time it didn't work. Somehow he died. I would say by Will's hand." I took Me-Maw's hand in mine. She was shaking all over. Knowing her own kith and kin had done such a thing. Even to someone as killable as Armand DuBois.

"They buried his body in the shed at the back of Cousin Leticia's lot. But then, later, Cousin Leticia becomes very religious. I think she intended to turn herself and maybe even Will in for what had happened to Armand DuBois. I think it's quite possible she told Will about her intentions. At the family reunion at Sabine Park, Will doped Leticia's Big Red with Seconal. When she got tired, Me-Maw and the rest of us talked her into going to lie down in the car. Will followed her and released wasps into the closed car, knowing his mother was deathly allergic to them. I think she woke up at some point, probably from all the stings, and tried to get out of the car, but it was too late. She died at the hospital."

We were all huddled together now, Paw-Paw with his arm around Me-Maw, Aunt Adele on the other side of Paw-Paw, holding his hand tightly. Ho stood nearby, and I had no idea if he understood anything I was saying, but by the look on his face, I could see he knew things were not good.

"Everything would have been fine for Will," I told Sheriff Bullet, "except that I found the jar he'd kept the wasps in in Cousin Leticia's car. There were two dead wasps still in it. They had obviously died before he released the others."

I sighed. "I'm the cause of Dorisca Judice's death," I told the sheriff. He raised an eyebrow, Pucci-style, but I hurried on. "I started investigating and trying to get the police interested. I decided this all had to do with Armand DuBois—which it did, but not the way I had it figured. Anyway, when I told Dorisca Judice that there was a possibility Letica had been murdered, I think she then tried to blackmail Will. She must have seen him tampering with the Big Red. That's all I can figure out. It wasn't until I saw that skeleton in the shed that I realized Armand DuBois had been dead for nearly fifteen years and that I'd been chasing a ghost." I sighed. "The only thing I can't figure out," I said, "is how Will knew we'd be at Cousin Leticia's house today."

Me-Maw whimpered. A pitiful sound. "Me. I tole him. I call his house this morning and make a message on his machine and I say we gonna go to Leticia's see what kinda damage, he wanna come?" She looked at me, tears streaming down her face. "If Mr. Sal he die it gonna be all my fault!"

I took the big old lady in my arms. "No, Me-Maw. It's Will's fault. Not anyone else's. And Pucci's gonna be fine. Just fine."

From my lips to God's ears.

꩜ Fifteen minutes later two things happened: The doctor came out of surgery to tell us Pucci was going to make it and Sheriff Bullett's deputy came back to say Will was gone.

"He can't be gone!" I argued. "He was totally unconscious when we left him!"

"You tie him up?" the sheriff asked.

I shook my head. "There wasn't time. We had to get Pucci to the hospital." I shook my head again. "There just wasn't time."

We found a Quality Inn about five miles outside of Armentine and got two double rooms and a cot to fit us all, girls in one, boys in the other. By the next day, Buddy Don Keehoe had arrived and was kicking butt and taking names. Pucci had taken three pints of blood and there was some muscle damage, but the bullet hadn't hit the bone. He was going to live. The doctor told him he'd have to do some squeezing exercises to get his grip back in his left hand. After the doctor left, Pucci had some suggestions on what he could squeeze. I dissuaded him from his ideas.

Somebody needed to go back to Port Arthur and gather up clothes and sundry to get the group through the days Pucci was in the hospital. Nobody, but nobody, was going to leave with the Italian stallion still hurt. I volunteered to go, which brought on an entire barrage of objections.

Pucci: "Your sexy cousin's still out there somewhere, Kruse. How stupid are you?"

Paw-Paw: "I go but this damn leg . . . Girl, you can't go by your own self—"

Me-Maw: "I go with her. That Willard he try to get me just watch some stuff, I tell you what!"

So we left late that afternoon, Me-Maw and I, taking the van and heading back to Port Arthur. We were going to have to be in Armentine for at least four days, because that's how long it would take before the doctors released Pucci. We had the key to Aunt Adele's house, and the combination, supplied by Pucci, on how to open the door of Ho's Scenic Cruiser. It consisted of turning the handle quickly clockwise, and just as quickly counterclockwise while standing on one leg and whistling the chorus of "Onward, Christian Soldiers."

The drive from Armentine to Port Arthur took a little less than a hour and a half with a good tailwind and no cops to witness my seventy-mile-an-hour cruising speed. I kept the window on the driver's side open, so I only caught every other word Me-Maw had to say. Which was a blessing.

We went first to the Groves and picked up Me-Maw's things, then passed by Aunt Adele's to pack her things.

It was close to seven o'clock when we finally got to the marina. I knew I'd be driving to Armentine in the dark, especially if I did as I planned and stopped at the Vietnamese restaurant I'd seen in Orange on the way back for dinner. I figured if Me-Maw didn't like it, she could wait in the van.

After three weeks, I'd had just about as much familial bliss as I could stand.

When we got to the marina, I told Me-Maw to pack up Paw-Paw's and my things and I went to get Ho's. It took a full five minutes to open the door of the Scenic Cruiser. The chorus to "Onward, Christian Soldiers" didn't work. It may have been that I'm not much of a whistler. I tried humming Jagger's "Beast of Burden," and that seemed to do the trick. The door opened and I went in and packed up some things for Ho and a change of clothes and some underwear for Pucci.

I dumped Pucci's and Ho's things in the van with Me-Maw's and Aunt Adele's and headed to Paw-Paw's shack to check on how Me-Maw's packing was going. She does get obsessive and I rethought my decision to let her go willy-nilly through my things. I also wondered if I'd packed my diaphragm. I was pretty sure I had—but also pretty sure Me-Maw wouldn't know what it was.

A peacock was standing in front of the porch and seemed disinclined to allow me entrance. I told him to move and he told me something very obscene in peacockese. I tried charging him but he just charged me back, causing me to make a quick run and hop for the van. He stood outside the van door, reading me the peacock riot act until he got bored. Which took a lot longer than a rational person would think. Looking at my watch, I knew it was going to be good and dark before I ever hit Louisiana, even if I didn't stop for dinner.

After my fine-feathered friend finally left, I got out and ran into the shack. And straight into the arms of Cousin Will.

*   *   *

He grabbed my arm and threw me onto the dilapidated old sofa, knocking the breath out of me. I lay there trying to catch my breath, trying to come up with a way to reason with him. And wondering where in the hell my grandmother was.

He leaned over me, breathing in my face. Strangely enough, he hadn't turned into an ogre. He was still as beautiful as ever. "You bitch!" he yelled, his breath knocking against my face like a physical force. It smelled strongly of Bourbon.

I tried to sit up. "Will, listen—"

He pushed me back down. "Shut up, bitch. I'll do the talking."

I nodded my head. "Okay—"

"I said shut up!" He screamed the words.

Good, I thought. Let him scream loud and long. Someone will hear him. Someone will rescue me.

He must have been reading my thoughts, because he said, "Don't worry. No one's gonna hear what goes on in here. Hardly anybody's back since the storm. I've had the whole place to myself for two days."

"Will, please, we have to talk—"

He pulled me up by my hair but since there was very little of it, it slipped out of his grasp. The momentum got me up, however, and I made a beeline for the door.

He was quicker than I. He caught me around the waist and threw me against Paw-Paw's kitchen table, knocking over the toaster and a coffee cup I hadn't washed before our rush to Me-Maw's house. Both fell to the floor, the toaster bouncing, the coffee cup breaking into a zillion shards.

He held me up against the wall, pressed close to me, his face only millimeters from mine, his body pressed against mine.

That's when I saw Me-Maw. She was lying on the floor

behind the sofa, her feet sticking out behind it—all of her that I could see. I almost screamed. My me-maw—dead. Lying there in a bloody heap—and then I saw one of her sensibly clad feet move. She was alive. Me-Maw was alive.

The panic that had almost gripped me at seeing my grandmother sprawled helplessly on the floor abated when I realized she was not dead. At that point all I felt was indignation. How dare he. I knew the fear wasn't far off, but I didn't think about it. I knew now was the time for rational thought. Now was the time to figure out how to get my grandmother and myself out of this mess. He was drunk, he was scared, he was angry beyond rational thought. In its own way, that was good. That left him open for manipulation.

I put a sneer on my face. "Okay," I said, "if you're gonna kill me, do it now. Right here. You're not gonna make me go anyplace with you. Do it right here."

I wanted out of that shack. I wanted to get in the van and drive. I couldn't help Me-Maw if I was dead in the shack. Outside I had a chance to get her help. Even if he still had the gun and even if he held it on me, getting out of the camp was still my best shot. Excuse the expression.

He grabbed my arm and pushed me toward the door. "You're gonna do what I tell you, bitch, when I tell you to do it. Get in the goddamn van. Now!"

He shoved me out the door. Lord, how I would have loved to see that peacock again. But he was nowhere in sight.

Will grabbed my arm again on the porch and walked me roughly to the passenger-side door of the van. Opening it, he shoved me in first, telling me to drive, and sat in the passenger seat next to me. The gun was back in his hand, aimed vaguely at my midsection. In retrospect I thought it would have been nice if we'd thought to pick up the gun before we headed for the hospital with Pucci. Hindsight is always twenty-twenty.

He directed me out of the marina and onto Highway 87 heading into town. That was good, I thought. First red light, I bail.

Naturally we didn't hit a red light until we were in downtown Port Arthur. There wasn't another car in sight. No one on the street. If I took that moment to bail out of the car, he'd shoot me before I got ten feet. The thought was moot, though, since he instructed me to go through the red light without slowing down. Which also would have been good if there had been a cop around to see. Which there wasn't.

On the other side of downtown we hit the refineries—lit up like Christmas trees all around us. Even with the windows shut and the air-conditioning on, the noise was deafening. Huge onion tanks and cooling towers with steam coming out surrounded us.

We got to the light on Highway 82 and Will told me to turn left. My stomach sank when I realized our destination. Highway 82 only went one way from there—over the Martin Luther King Bridge onto Pleasure Island. Dark, deserted, lonely Pleasure Island. I was hoping that after the hurricane of only a few days before, the island—the area to have received the most damage from the storm—would be closed. No such luck. The bridge loomed before us—open and going straight up into the sky. At that point I wasn't sure which I was more afraid of—Will's gun pointed at my ribs or that bridge that went straight up for a thousand miles and then made an improbably sharp right-hand turn in the middle before heading back down to earth, so far, far away.

I hadn't been to Pleasure Island in years. What had been the Coney Island of Port Arthur in the first half of the century, up to the 1950s, had been, when I knew it, a deserted stretch of island that ran for miles in either direction—from Louisiana back to the Neches River. There were any number of places to hide a body on Pleasure Island. A body that might never be found.

We turned right once we were off the bridge and, lo and behold, there were people—lots and lots and lots of people. Cars everywhere. Music. Ferris wheels. Bright lights.

"Shit," Will said. "I thought they canceled that 'cause of the storm."

"What is it?" I asked.

"Shrimp Fest," he said. "If you'd been cooperative, we could be there right now. Drinking beer, playing games. Watching the show. But no, not Kimmey Kruse, Girl Scout! You gotta stick your nose—"

I'd been moving the van toward the park, toward the cars and lights and people.

Will grabbed the wheel. "Bitch! Stay on the road. Keep going!"

I could have bailed then. I should have bailed then. But trying to maneuver the car toward the park had gotten Will's attention totally on me. He'd shoot me before I had the door partially open.

I kept driving. We passed the Coast Guard station, then a marina with sailboats and expensive houses and a country-club-type thing and a swanky beer joint, all grouped around the lagoon, the still pond with the seawall, on the other side of which is the Gulf of Mexico.

I saw in front of me one last turnoff toward the seawall on the far side of the lagoon. Beyond that the road stretched out into the marshes for ever and ever.

I turned the car a sharp ninety degrees, hitting the accelerator as hard as I could. Will was thrown off balance as I raced the car toward the seawall. I slammed on my brakes, throwing Will against the dashboard. Even with the brakes, the van slammed into the seawall, finally coming to a complete stop. I jumped out of the vehicle and ran as fast as I could to the lagoon.

The heavy cloud cover made the night bright with reflected lights. That was good for me in that I could see where I was going. It was bad in that Will could see where I was going. He had recovered quickly from his experience with the dashboard and was fast on my heels.

There was no one and nothing on this side of the lagoon. Running, I took stock of my options. I could run back to the road—but Will would catch me. His legs were longer. He could outrun me. Or I could go for the seawall. Maneuvering the seawall would put Will at a disadvantage. Speed would not be a winning factor in navigating the seawall—agility would be.

I ran for the wall and clambered up. Waist-high on a normal person, it was chest-high on me. Barely looking down, I ran along the wall until there was water on both sides of me—the Gulf on my left, choppy with strong currents, the lagoon on my right. Not being able to help myself, I stopped and turned my head. Will was behind me—maybe one hundred feet—but he was on his hands and knees, crawling as fast as he could toward me. I turned quickly forward, almost losing my balance, steadied myself and speed-walked on two feet along the narrow rim of the seawall.

Until I got to that part I'd forgotten about. That fifty-foot-wide gap where the boats from the marina were able to navigate in and out of the lagoon. I stopped dead. Turning around, I spied Will—now more like two hundred feet behind me—but coming fast.

Nothing to it but to do it. I dived into the lagoon. The currents at the gap were strong, pulling me toward the open water of the Gulf. For the first time that night, panic nearly gripped me. I'm a strong swimmer, but I'm small. I wasn't sure my ninety-five pounds could match the strength of the currents. But I beat the water into submission, plowing ahead as fast as possible, until I got to the other side of the gap. There was no way from the lagoon side to get back up on the seawall. On the Gulf side there were steps all along the wall leading down into the water—for fishing. Holding on tightly to the top of the wall, I hand-walked my way to the Gulf side, pulling myself up the steps with my hands and ninety-five pounds of "I ain't gonna die in Port Arthur" determination.

Once back on the wall, I looked back. Will was nowhere to be seen. But I could hear him. I could hear the engine of the van spring to life.

The swanky beer joint was closed due to hurricane damage. The country-club-type place was locked up tight. There were no cars and no lights around the condos or the houses. Most people had left the island before the storm, having not yet returned to their damaged homes.

I thought about breaking into one of the houses or condos and using the phone to call the police. But I figured the electricity and phone services were probably still out on the island. The only lights on the island I'd seen had been the ones at the Shrimp Fest, and those were probably coming from generators hauled in for the occasion.

I knew better than to go by the main road. Will would be patrolling that in the van. I could see the lights of the Shrimp Fest over the trees and headed into the bushes and through the woods, toward the lights.

Right smack-dab into the marsh. My high-tops sank into the mush up to my knees and salt-grass stalks reached higher than my head. My first thought was quicksand, but after near panic, I was able to pull myself up and onward. Then I thought of Paw-Paw's stories about snakes.

That's when I screamed. It made me feel so much better, I continued to scream all the way through the marsh. I doubted if Will could hear me—so much noise was coming from the Shrimp Fest that one little woman screaming in the marsh wasn't going to be heard above the rest of it.

I came out of the marsh and trees right at the parking lot of the park where the Shrimp Fest was being held. There were about a million cars. Lots of them vans. In the dark, I couldn't tell one van from another. So I avoided all vans, keeping my head low (which isn't hard), and ran toward the light and noise of the festival.

There was a man taking tickets at the entrance, but it was too late and he was too drunk to pay much attention to me as I slipped by him and headed into the crowds of the Shrimp Fest. People were everywhere—some wearing silly foam-rubber hats in the shape of shrimp and crawfish—everyone eating and with a beer in their hands. I knew there had to be security; in the 1990s, wherever two or more people gathered, someone hired a security guard. That's whom I was looking for. I rounded the corner next to a Pitch-a-Penny booth and ran straight into Cousin Will.

He grabbed my hair. I pulled back, losing him instantly, and started running as fast as I could. Twenty feet ahead of me I saw Buddy Don Keehoe with a shrimp on a stick and a beer. I screamed.

"Buddy Don! It's him! It's Will DuBois!"

Buddy Don whirled around and grasped the situation immediately. I was impressed. He went for something behind his back—his off-duty gun, I reasoned—but before he even had it out, Will fired, knocking Buddy Don to the ground. No one noticed—except the woman with Buddy Don. I ran away from them, trying to keep Will from firing again.

I knew if I ran any farther, I'd be off the park grounds and there'd be no way to get away from Will then. I stopped and whirled, pointing at Will only feet behind me. "He's got a gun!" I yelled at the top of my voice.

Now an interesting note about Texas, and Port Arthur in particular. There are a lot of bumper stickers in Texas that say, "You can have my gun when they pry my cold, dead fingers off it" and "Register criminals, not guns." My me-maw has her traveling gun—the one she carries in her purse whenever she goes to Beaumont or other places outside of Port Arthur 'cause you just never know what could happen to a woman on her own. Aunt Adele has her shower gun and Paw-Paw has about ten assorted firearms.

Which explains what happened next. When I screamed, eight people whirled around, six of them women, and all with guns in their hands, all pointed at Will DuBois. He stopped. I stopped. They stopped. Even the music stopped.

A big hand grabbed Will by the shoulder. I looked up and saw Buddy Don Keehoe, one arm bent at the elbow and held close to his body, a woman's scarf tied around it and dripping blood.

He turned Will toward him and said, "Will DuBois, you are under arrest. You have the right to remain silent, you have the right to try to run and get shot to shit by all these fine people here, you have the right to an attorney—"

I grabbed Buddy Don's good arm. "Call an ambulance!" I yelled. "Get them to Rainbow Marina fast."

Four days later we were gathered around the largest table on Dominque's deck. Everybody was there: Me-Maw, her head still bandaged but out of any danger from her concussion, Aunt Adele, Paw-Paw and Ho, and Pucci with his arm in a sling. Buddy Don Keehoe was there too, comparing gunshot wounds with Pucci. He'd had his interview with Cousin Will.

I'd been right almost all along the line. Armand had come back demanding money, Buddy Don said, and the only money in the house was the money Leticia had been working two jobs for to put Will through college. Will, home from college for the weekend, was the one who killed his father, by hitting him over the head with a chair. And Leticia, in her righteous way, had felt it necessary to tell Will that she planned on turning them both in at this late date for the murder of his father.

"But surely he'd have gotten off after all these years?" I said. "He was only a boy when it happened!"

"Um-hum," Buddy Don said, "more 'n likely. Lousiana law's different from Texas law, but all the same, bet he'da got off. Told him that, too. Know what he said?"

"What?" Pucci and I both asked.

"He said, 'Yeah, but I coulda lost my job!' "

I was right about Dorisca, too. She had seen him lacing Leticia's Big Red, and after I made my big announcement, had called Will and threatened him with exposure. But not for money.

"Seems this was one horny old broad," Buddy Don said. "Said she could be real nice to Will if he wanted her to. Said he could move into her house and live with her."

Pucci shuddered in the heat of a Port Arthur afternoon. "What else could he do but kill her?" he said.

I hit him on his good arm.

I went by What a Hoot that day to pick up my stuff. They weren't happy with me for missing so much work. They were talking about suing me. I laughed. I mentioned blood, turnips, things like that. I also mentioned my high-powered attorney, Phoebe R. Love. They mentioned I never darken their doors again.

On the fifth day, post-discharge, the whole group was at the airport to see Pucci off to Chicago, by way of Houston.

I walked with him alone toward the door leading to the tarmac. "We never did have our little talk," he said.

I sighed. "What's to say, Pucci? You live in Chicago, I live in Austin. Long-distance romances are a real drag, you know?"

"I thought women liked to talk about feelings, not practicality," he said.

"There you go again," I said, "stereotyping."

He grinned. "Yeah? Well, how's this for stereotypical Italian behavior?"

And with that and his good arm, he lifted me up and kissed me, with tongue this time. When he set me back down I was a quivering romance-novel heroine. Quivering, undulating, throbbing, and every other adjective imaginable.

The kiss was so good I almost didn't hear the applause coming from my relatives less than ten feet away.

Pucci grinned and headed for the door to the tarmac. "See you in the funny papers, Kruse."

" 'Bye, Pucci," I said, probably not loud enough for him to hear. I was having difficulty with my throat, as well as my legs and internal organs.

⟡ Two days later I was back at the airport, this time for my own plane to Austin for more clothes before I headed off for Altoona, Pennsylvania, for a two-day gig at a small club there. Paw-Paw still wasn't able to drive himself or be totally on his own, but that was okay. Since he was moving back in with Me-Maw. Ain't love grand?

Epilogue

I DROVE WITH MY PARENTS TO PORT ARTHUR FOR THANKSGIVING that year. Me-Maw'd had a goose killed and made two tons of dirty-rice dressing for the occasion. We were in the house for no more than fifteen minutes when she told me the news about Cousin Barbara Sue's husband, Jimmy Lynn. Seemed he got caught in a ménage à quintet in a raid at the All-Nude Asian Massage Parlor way out on Beaumont Highway a month before. According to Me-Maw, who got the news from her daughter, my aunt Cynthia, Barbara Sue had kicked him out of the house and was having the church records gone over by an auditor. I decided to go see her before dinner started.

"I don't know if I'll be able to keep it," she said, staring dreamily at the four-thousand-square-foot dream home, "but the kids and I'll be fine even if it's in a trailer park somewhere."

I smiled. "You'll do great, Barbara Sue."

She grinned back at me. "Especially after I take that son of a bitch to the cleaner's. He'll be lucky if I leave him a blow-dryer."

She sighed, looked down at her hands and back up at me. "One thing, though—Melissa will turn eighteen next year."

I nodded. Melissa—the little girl lost.

"I contacted ALMA, that agency that helps birth parents and adopted children find their birth families. I put my name on the list. It could take a while, maybe never. But it's time to try."

I hugged her and said, "That's the best idea I've heard lately."

Aunt Laurina had been invited to Thanksgiving Dinner. Me-Maw had told me on the phone that all the women in the family, all three generations, were to gather after dinner to talk about Blanche and Armand DuBois. She'd decided, after everything that had happened, that secrets were something to be shared within the family. I hoped Barbara Sue would take that opportunity to tell the family about Melissa. Different times, different ways.

After I left Barbara Sue's house I headed out to the bridge for a quick visit with Paw-Paw before dinner. Me-Maw, of course, had kicked him out again and he wasn't invited to share Thanksgiving. But that's the way it goes.